TALES AFTER TEA

by

ENID BLYTON

COLLINS

LONDON AND GLASGOW

This Impression 1967

© *Enid Blyton*

PRINTED AND MADE IN GREAT BRITAIN BY
WM. COLLINS SONS AND CO. LTD.
LONDON AND GLASGOW

CONTENTS

THE KING OF THE CASTLE

THE CHILDREN thought they would build the biggest sand-castle that had ever been built on the beach before.

"It shall be higher than any of us," said Benjy.

"Taller than the chair-man," said Irene. The chair-man was very tall—taller than anyone the children had ever seen.

"Gracious!" said Kathie. "It *will* be an enormous castle. We'll all help to build it, then it will soon be done."

"Don't let's ask Arthur to help," said Benjy. "He's so big and rough."

"But he's strong and he could build very fast," said Irene.

"All the same, don't let's ask him," said Kathie. "He shouts so, and he always wants the best of everything for himself."

"All right, we won't ask him," said Benjy. "William! Peter! Joan! Come and help us. We are going to build the biggest castle that has ever been seen on this beach."

The six children set to work. The castle began to take shape. They patted it down well as they built it. It was to be really grand and very strong. Soon Arthur came down on the beach and hurried to the castle.

"I'll help," he said.

"We don't really need any more help, Arthur," said Kathie, politely.

Arthur gave her a rough push. "I shall help if I want to. You girls aren't much good at digging. Silly little girl-spades you have! Look at mine— real iron!"

Nobody said much to Arthur as he helped to dig the castle. He was a big boy, though he wasn't much older than the others. He was very rough, and nobody dared to say no to him in case he pushed them over.

The castle grew bigger and bigger. Soon it was taller than the children, even taller than Arthur. The chair-man came over to look at it.

"It will soon be taller than I am!" he said, with a laugh.

"We hope it will," said Benjy. "That's just what we said when we planned to build it—we said we'd make it even taller than you!"

At last the children were too tired to dig any more. They put down their spades and looked at their castle. It was certainly the biggest they had ever seen anywhere.

It had a big moat round it, which had a little water in for paddling. The children had made steps up the side of the castle, and had flattened the top so that one or two of them could sit there.

"You girls can go up and sit on the top of the castle if you like," said William. But Arthur wasn't going to have that! What—*girls* on the top of that fine castle!

"Oh, no," he said. "*I'm* going to be king of this castle. It's wasted on girls. I'm the biggest of you, and I shall be king."

"No, Arthur," said Benjy. "That's not fair. Let the girls sit on it."

"If you say any more I'll knock the whole castle down!" said Arthur, in a rage. Everyone stared at him. They knew he would do as he said if they tried to prevent him from doing what he wanted. What a horrid boy he was!

Joan began to cry. Benjy took her hand and pulled her away from the castle. "Come on," he said to the others, "we don't want it knocked down after we've spent so long in building it—but I'm not going to stay and see Arthur being king! I've got some money. I'll buy two ice-creams and share them with you."

Arthur grinned to himself when he saw the other children going off. As usual, he had got his own way. Now he could be king of the castle!

He climbed up the steps the children had made in the side of the enormous castle. He sat himself down on the top. The sea was almost up to the castle now, for the tide was coming in. What fun he would have when the first wave splashed into the moat! He would stay on the castle for a long time and then paddle to the shore.

The chair-man had seen all that had happened. He didn't like Arthur.

"If you were my boy I'd spank you," he said to Arthur. "Always spoiling things for the others!"

"I'll throw your chairs into the sea!" said Arthur, in a temper. The chair-man looked at

Arthur with scorn, and then went to give tickets
to some people up the beach who had just sat
down on two of his chairs.

Arthur was left alone on the big castle. The
other children were buying ice-creams up on the
parade. There was hardly anyone on the beach.
Arthur was sorry, because he wanted lots of people
to look at him and think how grand he was sitting
on the top of the most enormous castle that had
ever been built of sand.

"I'm the king of the castle!" he sang in a very loud voice. "I'M THE KING OF THE CASTLE!"

Nobody took any notice of him at all. They just thought he was silly.

The sea swept all round the castle. Arthur laughed with joy. "You can't eat my castle yet!" he shouted to the waves. "It's too big and strong. Ah, yes—you can try to splash my toes if you like! It will take you a long time to get me, for I'm so high up!"

Certainly the castle was very, very strong indeed. The sea couldn't seem to gobble it up quickly, as it usually gobbled every other castle. It swirled round it, and then the waves ran far up the beach. The tide was in properly now. Suddenly Arthur saw a very big wave indeed coming right at him. It splashed him from head to foot.

"Oh! You spiteful thing!" said Arthur, spitting the salt water out of his mouth. "It's time I paddled back to the shore if you're going to do things like that!"

He looked back towards the beach—and his heart sank in dismay. "Goodness! I'll never get back! The tide is right in, far behind the castle. I'm in the middle of the big sea!"

That's really what it looked like, for the sea was all round the castle, and had gone right up the beach, almost to the promenade. Arthur was frightened.

"Help!" he yelled. "Help!"

The other children heard him. They stared in surprise. "Gracious! Arthur's still on the castle, and the sea is as deep as can be all round it!" said Benjy. "He'll be drowned."

"You're king of the castle, aren't you? Well, command the sea to go back!" yelled William. Everyone laughed. Arthur began to cry.

"Baby!" shouted Irene. "Fancy a big boy like you crying. You always laugh at us for doing that. Baby!"

"Serves you right for sitting on the castle, instead of letting *us*," yelled Kathie.

"Oh, save me, save me!" shouted Arthur.

The children couldn't help being glad that Arthur was getting a fright—but all the same they didn't want him to be drowned. "We'd better call the chair-man," said Irene. "He's so tall that he can easily wade to the castle and save him."

So they called the chair-man and pointed out Arthur on the far-off sand-castle, which was now swiftly disappearing beneath the waves.

"Let him be," said the chair-man. "A wetting won't hurt him. Do him good."

"No, please rescue him," begged Joan, who was very tender-hearted. "Please, please do."

The chair-man liked Joan. "All right," he said, "I'll save him—but he doesn't deserve it!"

He rolled his trousers far above his knees and waded out to the castle, which was now almost beneath the waves. Arthur was standing on it, and he was very wet.

The chair-man grabbed him and took him into his arms. Arthur didn't even say thank you. He only grumbled because the man had been so long.

"Why didn't you come at once?" he complained. "I'm wet as can be."

"Well, if that's the way you are going to talk, you may as well get a little wetter!" said the chair-man, in a rage. And he dropped Arthur out of his arms, splash, into the sea. Goodness, what a shock he got! He had to scramble out of the water as best he could.

"And now, listen to me," said the tall chair-man

to the shivering boy. "Any more nonsense from you and I'll take you out to sea in a boat and drop you overboard. Do you hear that? Ho—king of the castle, indeed! I never heard such nonsense. You behave yourself in future!"

And Arthur does! A good thing, too, isn't it?

THE VERY SILLY BOY

THERE WAS once a very silly boy called Don. I don't know if you know anyone who just won't think, and who can't seem to remember to wipe his feet, or shut a door, or hang his coat up. Well, if you do, you'll know what Don was like—only he was much worse!

Don simply would *not* do things right. He didn't try to remember anything. If his father sent him to buy a paper he would come back after about an hour and ask what it was his father had sent him out for. And if his mother asked him to take his boots to the cupboard and put the kettle on the stove, he would be sure to put the kettle in the cupboard and his boots on the stove to cook.

"You're a donkey!" his father would say half-a-dozen times a day. "Yes, you are! You can do the things you want to all right—you spend hours sorting out your stamps and putting them into your book most beautifully. You carve away at that little ship of yours, and never do a thing wrong to it. But as soon as you have to do anything for anybody else, what happens? You behave like a silly donkey and do everything wrong, or else forget all about it."

"I'll try to be better," promised Don. But he never once kept his promise. His mother and father, and his teacher, too, gave him hundreds of chances—but he just wouldn't try.

And then one day Don got a terrible shock. His father called him to him and looked closely at his face.

"I'm afraid, I'm very much afraid that you really are going to turn into a donkey," he said, sadly. "Well, well, it can't be helped, I suppose. Perhaps I shouldn't have called you Don—that's half of Don-key. Mother, don't give Don that stew for his dinner. He'd be far better to have raw carrots. Those are very good for donkeys."

"Very well," said Don's mother, and she rang the bell for Mary, the housemaid. "Mary, bring a dish of raw carrots, please," she said. And in a minute or two in came the raw, red carrots.

Don stared at them and then sniffed at the stew. It smelt so good. "Daddy," he said. "I know this is a joke! I know you're cross because I forgot to do my homework last night. I'm not really a donkey! I can't eat raw carrots."

But, to Don's horror, neither Daddy nor Mother smiled at all. They just looked very sad and very serious.

"You're wrong, Don," said Daddy. "This isn't a joke. I'm afraid you're much more of a donkey than we thought you were. We always hoped you would grow out of your silly ways and be a real, proper boy. But it's no good. We shall have to treat you like a donkey. Now, go out into the garden and eat your raw carrots. Be a good donkey!"

"I can't eat carrots!" cried Don, in fright, bursting into tears. "I won't!"

"Well, go into the field at the bottom of the garden and try the thistles," said his father, in a serious voice. "Donkeys love those. They may seem a bit prickly at first, but your mouth will soon grow used to them. Run along now."

And, to Don's horror, his father pushed him out of doors, and wouldn't let him come back! He thought he must be in a dream. He looked down at himself. Surely he *wasn't* growing like a donkey? He put his hands to his head and felt his ears. Were they growing long? He stood and thought for a long time.

"Daddy is mean to treat me like a donkey," he

said, and he stamped his foot. The gardener heard him, and looked up from where he was digging.

"Hallo, what are *you* stamping about?" he said. "Do you think you are a horse or a donkey, stamping about like that?"

Don went pale. Goodness! Here was the gardener talking in the same way as Daddy. He began to cry again. "Daddy says I'm such a donkey that I'm to be treated like one," he said to the gardener. "He gave me raw carrots to eat, and said I must go and try the thistles over there. But I'm NOT a donkey."

"Well, only donkeys behave as stupidly as you, surely," said the gardener. "They just don't use their brains, and if people try to make them do something they don't understand or like they start to kick and stamp. Oh, yes—you're very like a little donkey. I should go and eat those raw carrots if I were you. It might be better to be a good donkey than a bad boy."

Don didn't dare to go indoors. He stayed outside, very hungry, till he heard the school-bell ringing. Then Daddy called him.

"You needn't go to school. Donkeys can't learn anything. You can go for a scamper round the thistle-field if you like."

Well, it was carpentry and gym that afternoon

at school, and Don didn't want to miss those. So he decided he would go. He just wasn't going to be a donkey, no matter what anyone said!

When he came home to tea there was a plate of raw carrots for him again. Don looked at his father and mother. His voice shook, but he said what he had made up his mind to say.

"I know I've been silly. I know I've never tried to do things properly, unless I wanted to. I know I've behaved like a donkey. But please, I don't want to be treated like one, Daddy and Mother. Give me one more chance to be a boy, and I do really promise to make you proud of me. Just one more chance. Then if I begin to behave like a donkey again I'll eat the carrots and go and sleep in the shed."

"Spoken like a man!" said his Daddy, looking as pleased as he could be. "Not a bit like a donkey! Well, Mother, what do you say? Do we give him one more chance? Just one? After all, he doesn't look or speak like a donkey now—he's spoken like a stout little fellow!"

"Of course he shall have one more chance," said Mother, taking away the carrots and putting a pile of potted-meat sandwiches in front of Don. "We'll see what happens. And, Daddy, what about calling him by his real name of Donovan, not Don? It sounds such a fine, manly name, not a bit like a donkey. It will help him to remember."

So now Don is Donovan—and, my word, didn't he take his last chance well! You'd never think he was the same boy. But there's just one thing he will never, never eat in a salad or a stew. Do you know what that is? Guess! Yes—carrots!

BILLY-BOB AND THE FARM

ONCE MOTHER promised to take Billy-Bob and Belinda for a day at Mrs. Johnson's farm. It was a lovely place, with white ducks on a pond, red cows in the fields, and grey sheep all over the hills.

And just when the day came for them to go, and the sun shone out warm and golden on the buttercups, Belinda was ill!

Her throat hurt her, and her nose sniffed all the time.

"Darling, what a bad cold you've got!" said Mother. "You'll have to stay in bed."

"But, Mother, you did say you'd take me and Billy-Bob to the farm!" wept poor Belinda.

"Yes, I know. But you can't possibly go with such a bad cold," said Mother. "You'll give it to everyone else."

"Oh, I promise I won't," said Belinda. "I'll keep it all to myself, Mother—really I will."

"You might give it to the ducks and the chickens and the cows," said Billy-Bob, solemnly. "Then they would go sneezing all over the place, Belinda."

That made Belinda laugh. But when Mother had tucked her up into bed she began to cry again, because she really did feel so miserable. Billy-Bob hated to see her crying.

"I'm not going to the farm, either," he said, taking her hot little hand. "I shall wait till you can go. Then we'll go together."

"Billy-Bob, I keep thinking of the white ducks swimming on the blue pond, and the little lambs skipping," said poor Belinda, wiping her nose and her eyes. "I did so badly want to see them to-day. Really I did."

Mother called Billy-Bob. "Billy-Bob! Leave Belinda for a little while, and see if she will go to sleep. I want you to go and fetch me some soap from the grocer's."

Billy-Bob patted Belinda's hand and left her. But before he went downstairs to see Mother he ran into his own bedroom and took down his money-box. He emptied it out. There was a whole shilling there, and four pennies. Billy-Bob put them into his pocket. He meant to buy something for Belinda.

He set off with a basket. First he went to the grocer's and got the soap for Mother. Then he went across to the toy-shop. He looked into the window for a very long time. Everything seemed very dear indeed. If only he had five shillings he could buy that lovely baby-doll whose eyes were so blue. If he had two shillings and sixpence he could buy a bear that wound up and danced.

Then he saw a lovely little farm, with animals in the farmyard. Oh, how Belinda would love that! There was no price on it, so perhaps it would only cost one shilling and fourpence. He hurried inside.

"Please, how much is that farmhouse and farm-yard and animals?" he asked the shop-girl.

"Twelve shillings and sixpence, if you want everything there," said the girl. "There are cows, sheep, ducks, and chicks, and a dog as well."

"Oh dear! I've only got a shilling and four-pence," said Billy-Bob, sadly.

"Well, did you specially want a farm?" said the girl. "I've got lots of other things you can have for that price. A tiny doll; a book; a dolls' house chest-of-drawers; a little musical box . . ."

"Belinda's got all those things," said Billy-Bob. "I did very specially want a farm for her because, you see, she was going to visit Mrs. Johnson's farm to-day, and now she can't because she's in bed. So I thought that little farm would make up to her for being disappointed. But it's much too dear for me to buy."

"Well, *I* know what you can have," said the shop-girl, smiling all over her pink face. "Look— what about this book? It's got a farmhouse in— see? And fences. And a pond and animals and birds. They can all be cut out and stood up. It's simply lovely."

"Oooh," said Billy-Bob, pleased, "it does look nice. Yes, I'll have that. How much is it, please?"

"One shilling," said the girl, and she gave it to him. "Now you'll still have fourpence to put back into your money-box!"

Billy-Bob hurried home. He found a blunt pair of scissors, because Mother didn't let either him or Belinda use a sharp-pointed pair, and he ran upstairs to Belinda.

"Belinda! I've got a farm for you! Look!" He showed the book to Belinda, and she pouted her lip a little.

"It's not like a real farm!" she said.

"It will be when I've cut it out for you," said Billy-Bob. "Now cheer up, and just watch me! I'll get a big tray for you to put on your knees, and you can set the farm and all the animals on it as I cut them out for you."

He put the tray on the bed, and then began to

cut out all the pictures very carefully. He cut out beautifully, and gave each thing to Belinda as he finished it. First the big farmhouse, that folded round and made a proper house. Belinda set it up and found that she could even open the little paper door. Then the fences were cut out, and she set them round the farmhouse to make a proper farm-yard.

Then the blue pond and the old well were cut out, and Belinda put those where she wanted them in the yard. Then what an excitement—all the animals were cut out, and the ducks and chickens, the farm-dog and the farm-cat!

"Oh, Billy-Bob, it's beginning to look so real!" said Belinda, happily. "Cut out the farmer for me, and he shall stand beside his dog."

It was dinner-time before the farm was finished, and Mother cried out in surprise when she saw it all on the big tray. "Billy-Bob! Belinda! How perfectly lovely! Why, it's very like Mrs. Johnson's farm, with the well, and the pond—and all the animals and birds! Belinda, here is your dinner. I hope you feel hungry."

"I do, rather," said Belinda. "And my throat is much better. I just simply couldn't think of it when I was making my farm. Mother, isn't it lovely and *real*?"

T.A.T.   B

Belinda ate all her dinner. Then she was sleepy, so she lay down to rest. Billy-Bob put the big tray, with the farm on it, on the chest-of-drawers, where she could see it. Belinda lay looking at it.

Then a peculiar thing happened. It grew bigger—and bigger—and bigger! The house-door opened, and the farmer walked out, whistling! His dog jumped beside him. The ducks swam on the pond and began to quack. The cat jumped up on the roof of the farmhouse and began to clean itself.

"Oh!" said Belinda, sitting up. "Oh! It's all come real. It's big enough for me to go through the gate and see everything properly!"

She got out of bed and ran through the farm-yard-gate. The farmer picked her up and put her on his shoulder. "Come and see my fine cows!" he said. "You shall help me to milk them. And you shall feed the hens, too."

So Belinda sat on a milking-stool and milked a big cow, who mooed softly at her. The farmer gave her a drink of the warm, creamy milk, and it was most delicious.

Then he let her scatter corn for the hens, and, goodness me, how they came round her, peck-peck-pecking! "Oh, this is much better than Mrs. Johnson's farm!" cried Belinda. "I've never milked one of *her* cows. Oh, please, can I stroke your cat, Farmer? Do get her down from the roof for me and let me cuddle her. She's so big and soft."

But the cat wouldn't come down. The farmer went into the farmhouse and brought out a little ladder. Belinda ran up it to the roof—but, dear me, she missed her footing half-way up, and fell! Down she went, and down, and down—and landed with a bump! But not on the ground. No—on her bed!

Billy-Bob came into the room and looked at Belinda in surprise. "Why did you squeal out?" he said. "Were you dreaming?"

"No," said Belinda, rubbing her eyes. "I haven't slept a wink because something *most* exciting happened, Billy-Bob. The farm came alive! I went and visited it. I went through that farm-gate—look—and into the yard. It's all gone small again now—but it got properly big. And, oh, Billy-Bob, I milked that cow over there— and I fed the hens. Don't you think they look fatter?"

"It was all a dream!" said Billy-Bob, and he patted her plump little hand.

Belinda was cross. "It was *not*!" she said. "The cat jumped up on to the roof, and I wanted to stroke it, so the farmer got a ladder for me, and I fell off—into bed, somehow. And *look*, Billy-Bob —the cat is on the roof still! That just *shows* you I didn't dream it! Because you know quite well that we put the cat down on the ground beside the well before!"

That was quite true. Billy-Bob was really very puzzled. He simply didn't know whether Belinda had had a dream, or whether it was all really true!

You'd better cut out a farm next time you're in bed, and see if the same thing happens to you! If it does, don't forget to let me know!

THE GIRL WHO FOUND SIXPENCE

ONE MORNING when Jeanie was coming back from the shops she had a great surprise. There, lying on the pavement, was a shining silver sixpence!

"Good gracious!" said Jeanie, in delight. "I've found sixpence."

She picked it up—and then she remembered something. Mother had always said that if anything was found in the street, *somebody* must have lost it, and the finder must always try to give it back to the real owner.

"Oh, what a nuisance!" said Jeanie to herself. She looked round and about to see if anyone was looking for the sixpence. But nobody was. So she hurried away with it.

Round the next corner she met a little boy who was crying. His name was Kenneth. Jeanie was a kind little girl, and she almost went up to ask Kenneth what was the matter—and then she stopped.

"Suppose he is crying because he lost sixpence! I would have to give it back to him then. I shan't ask him what's the matter. Perhaps he's crying because his mother is cross with him—or maybe he has fallen down and hurt his knee."

So Jeanie hurried home, and didn't ask Kenneth why he was crying.

She didn't tell her mother about the silvery sixpence. She wanted to keep it a secret and spend it herself on anything she wanted.

"I shall buy lots and lots of sweets," thought Jeanie. "I shan't tell anyone I've got them. Just this once I'll eat them all myself."

So that afternoon she went to the sweet-shop and she bought two-pennyworth of cheap pink sweets, two-pennyworth of cheap green sweets, and two-pennyworth of cheap yellow sweets. They were the kind that mother didn't usually let her buy.

She went for a walk by herself, and she ate all the sweets, everyone. First she ate the green ones, then she ate the yellow ones, and last of all, she ate the pink ones. So you can see that she had a great feast.

When she got home she had a lovely surprise.

"Jeanie, Hilda has just been here to ask if you will go to her party to-morrow," said her mother. "Won't that be nice for you? I'll buy a new hair-ribbon and a sash to match."

Jeanie was most excited. "This is certainly my lucky day!" she said to herself. "First I find a sixpence—then I have heaps of sweets all to my-self—and then I'm asked to a party. Oh, how lovely!"

Now those sweets were cheap and nasty, and although a few of them would have been all right, three bags of them were bad for anybody. And in the middle of the night poor Jeanie woke up with a most dreadful pain in her tummy. She sat up and cried.

Her mother came to see what was the matter. "I've got such a pain," wept Jeanie. "It won't go. It's just here, Mummy."

Her mother gave her some horrid medicine to take, brought her a hot-water bottle, and told her to try and go to sleep. But the sweets gave her

such a tummy-ache that she couldn't go to sleep at all. In the morning she was pale and tired.

"You must stay in bed to-day, Jeanie," said her mother. "You look quite ill."

"Oh, Mummy! But I'm going to Hilda's party!" cried Jeanie.

"You can't possibly do that," said her mother. "I couldn't let you go out after a bad night like last night. You must lie in bed and rest to-day. Perhaps you will be well enough to get up to-morrow. I really can't think what has upset you. You had quite ordinary things to eat yesterday."

Jeanie remembered the pink, green, and yellow sweets, and she went red. She turned her face to her pillow so that her mother could not see how red she was. She knew quite well that she had a pain because of eating so many cheap sweets. Mummy had always warned her about that.

"I don't feel as if I could eat another sweet all my life long!" thought poor Jeanie. "I just feel really sick when I think of them. Oh dear—how greedy I was!"

She cried when she remembered Hilda's party. It was such a dreadful disappointment. Jeanie lay and thought about everything.

"It was all because I found that sixpence and kept it, without really trying to find out who had lost it," she thought. "I am sure it was Kenneth's. Instead of giving it to him I kept it and bought those nasty sweets with it, and ate them all greedily without offering anybody else any. Then they gave me a pain and made me miss Hilda's party. Oh, how unhappy I am!"

About half-past six that evening Mummy came into Jeanie's room with a smiling face.

"Hilda has just been along to give you something from her party," she said. "Look, here is a bag of sweets—all different colours!"

Jeanie took the bag and opened it. Inside were

some really beautiful sweets—green, pink, and yellow, just the same colours as those she had bought the day before, but much, much nicer sweets.

And poor Jeanie couldn't eat one! It made her feel sick just to look at them. "I don't want any," she said, miserably. "They make me feel ill."

Then she began to cry. Mummy sat down on the bed and looked at her.

"Is there anything you would like to tell me, Jeanie, dear?" she asked. "If there is anything worrying you I would like to know it—because mothers can usually put things right, you know. So do tell me."

"I will tell you," wept Jeanie. And she poured out the story about finding the sixpence, and not asking Kenneth if it was his, and buying the sweets and eating them all. Mummy listened to the whole story. Then she took Jeanie's hand.

"Don't worry about it any more," she said. "You can put it all right if you want to. It *was* Kenneth who lost the sixpence, because his mother told me how upset he was. Have you sixpence in your money-box?"

"Yes," said Jeanie, cheering up. "I could give him that. I wish I could make up for his unhappiness at losing the sixpence, too."

"Yes, it would be nice to do that," said Mummy.

"Oh, I know what I could do!" said Jeanie. "I could send him round the sweets, too, that Hilda brought me, couldn't I? He would love those. I was greedy with the others, but I shan't be with these! I won't keep even one for myself for to-morrow."

"That would be a good idea," said Mummy, pleased. "Kenneth would love the sweets. You shall take the sixpence and the sweets to him to-morrow."

"I wish I had given back the sixpence instead of

keeping it," said Jeanie. "It's brought me a lot of horrid things!"

"Yes, that's the worst of doing something mean," said Mummy. "Mean deeds always bring horrid things behind them. Never mind—you are going to make up for being mean, and that will put things right again. Your bad luck will go!"

And sure enough it did! Jeanie went round to see Kenneth, and took him a sixpence out of her

money-box and the bag of sweets, and told him
she was sorry she hadn't asked him if he had lost
the sixpence.

"How nice you are, Jeanie, to come and tell me
all this, and give me your own sixpence and
sweets," said Kenneth. "I'm having a birthday
party on Saturday. Will you come?"

Well, what do you think of that? Jeanie flew
home to tell her mother, as pleased as could be.
And you will be glad to know that there were
lovely sweets at Kenneth's party, too, and Jeanie
loved eating them!

THE CROSS OLD AUNTIE

ROBIN WAS feeling very sad. He had to say good-bye to his mother and father and go to live with old Aunt Katie. Mummy and Daddy were going away for a long time. "So, you see, we shan't be able to look after you for a little while," said Mummy. "And also we want to send you away into the country, where you will grow strong and big. So my old Aunt Katie says she will have you."

46

"Is she my great-aunt, then?" asked Robin. "Is she old and cross?"

"Well, she *is* rather old," said Mummy. "But as far as I remember she isn't cross. But you must be as good and as helpful as you can, and remember that old people are not so patient as we are. So be a good boy, won't you? We will come and see you as often as we can."

Robin wondered very much what Great-Aunt Katie would be like. She met him at the station. She was a tall, bent old lady with sharp eyes. She took Robin's hand.

"Welcome to our little village!" she said. "I hope you are going to be a good boy. I can't put up with bad ones."

Robin didn't like the sound of that much. He did mean to be as good as gold, but, after all, it was very difficult *always* to be good. And he certainly found it very, very hard at his great-aunt's!

Great-Aunt Kate didn't like him to sing or whistle. She was really DREADFULLY cross if he forgot to wipe his feet. And if he banged the door she nearly jumped out of her skin, and scolded him for quite ten minutes about it. Robin was always afraid he was going to do something he shouldn't do.

Great-Aunt Katie liked Robin to run down to the village for her, to get things she had forgotten. It was a very long way to the village, and Robin got very tired, especially when he had to go two or three times. But he was a good-hearted little boy, and didn't grumble.

One day he had to go to the village three times, and the last time he was so tired that he was very slow indeed when he was coming home. Great-Aunt Katie met him at the gate.

"Goodness me!" she said, "whatever have you been doing? You *have* been a long time! I've

Robin played about for a little while, putting pots inside one another, and setting out trowels, forks, and other things in a row. Then he wondered if there was anything nice under the heap of sacks. So he went to the end of the shed and tugged at them. He pulled them away, and then found something wrapped up in brown paper and tied with string. It was a most peculiar shape, and seemed to have three wheels at the bottom. Robin couldn't imagine *what* it could be.

"I'll just pull away the paper a bit and see," he thought. "It's really such a very strange shape." So he pulled away part of the paper, and, to his enormous surprise, he saw what looked like a long, hairy tail! Robin stared in astonishment. Then he pulled away the paper at the other end—and, lo and behold, a horse's head looked out at him! A wooden head with glass eyes and a mane!

"It's a horse on wheels!" thought Robin, beginning to feel excited. "It's very old. Most of the paint is off, and the mouth is a bit broken. How very queer that it should be here! It can't belong to Great-Aunt. She could never ride this little horse on wheels. It's just about *my* size!"

Well, you can guess that before long Robin had undone the horse, and, sure enough, it was a fine little horse on three big wheels, and it had pedals!

Robin got on the horse's back, put his feet on the pedals, and rode round the big shed on the horse! It ran quite easily on its three rubber-tyred wheels. It was marvellous!

54

Robin heard Great-Aunt Katie calling him. He went to see what she wanted. "Shake hands with Mrs. Brown and say good-bye," she said. So he did, very politely, for he had good manners. As soon as she had gone he turned to his old aunt.

"Aunt Katie! Did you know there was a horse in the shed?" he cried.

"A horse! Goodness me, how did it get there?" cried his aunt, in amazement. "Is it galloping round? Where did it come from? We must shoo it out at once."

"Not a *real* horse, Great-Aunt," said Robin, with a laugh. "A lovely little wooden horse on three wheels. I've been riding it. I hope it doesn't matter."

"Well, I'd forgotten all about that horse!" said Great-Aunt, surprised. "It once belonged to your uncle when he was a little boy like you. When he grew up I wrapped it away in paper, thinking maybe I could give it to a grandchild. But I've got no grandchildren after all—only a little great-nephew called Robin. Well, well— you'll have to have it, that's all. Would you like it?"

"Oh, Aunt Katie! Why, I'd like it better than anything in all the world!" said Robin, quite wild with delight. "It's much, much better than a tricycle. I really do feel as if I'm riding a horse when I'm pushing the pedals around. It goes awfully fast."

"Well, you have it, then," said the old lady. "You deserve it, because you're really a kind little boy, always running errands for me. I know I'm a cross old woman, but you mustn't mind that. I won't make you go that long walk down to the village too often again. Mrs. Brown was saying it's really too far for your little legs."

A wonderful idea came to Robin. He beamed at the old lady and took her hand. "Listen!" he said. "I'll go as often as you like—because I'll ride on the horse! It will only take me half the time if I ride the horse, and it will be such a treat to do it. I've never had a scooter or a tricycle—the horse is much, much nicer!"

"Well now, that *is* a good idea!" said his Great-Aunt, smiling, too.

"Can't you think of anything you want now, this very minute?" asked Robin. "I'll go down to the village on the horse and get it."

"But you've been three times to-day already," said the old lady.

"It would be a treat this time," said the little boy. So his aunt thought of the evening paper—

and Robin leapt on his wheeled horse and rode off to the village to get it. Wasn't he proud? Wasn't he pleased? How all the other children stared when they saw him on the fine little horse, pedalling away as fast as could be!

And now he and his cross old great-aunt are the very best of friends, and Robin doesn't mind *how* many times he goes down to the village each day. I wouldn't, either, if I had a horse like that to ride, would you?

WHAT A PITY!

JOCK LOOKED out of his nursery window one winter morning, and saw a blue spire of smoke rising up into the air.

"Look, Mummy," he cried, "gardener has made a bonfire!"

"So he has," said Mummy. "But just remember this, Jock—you are *not* to touch it. You can go and watch it burning, if you don't go too near— but you are certainly not to touch it in any way.

You burnt your coat last year, and I can't afford to buy you a new coat again *this* year!"

"All right, Mummy," said Jock. He felt in his pocket, and looked worried.

"What's the matter?" asked Mummy. "Have you lost something?"

Jock felt in the other pocket, and smiled. "No, it's all right," he said. "It was my postal-order for five shillings I was looking for. I want to go to the post-office and get five shillings for it, and buy a lovely blue aeroplane I saw in the toy-shop, Mummy. It really and truly flies."

"Well, well, what an extraordinary thing for an aeroplane to do!" said Mummy, with a laugh. "But, Jock, please don't have that paper money loose in your pocket. You will lose it. Put it into your purse with your pennies. It will be safe there."

Jock's purse was in the night-nursery. He couldn't be bothered to fetch it just then! "I'll get it in a minute," he said.

Well, you know what that means—it means that it won't be done! And, of course, Jock quite forgot to put his paper money in his purse. He went out to play in the garden with his postal-order crammed into his coat-pocket.

He went to see the bonfire. The gardener was

there, raking dead leaves on to it, and throwing on rotten old sticks and the stems of cut-down plants.

"I wish I could do that," said Jock.

"Now, don't you dare to do anything of the sort," said the gardener at once. "Just don't you dare, my boy! Didn't you burn your coat last year on my bonfire? And didn't I get into trouble for letting you go too close? You go right away, please."

"Oh, gardener, just let me stay here and watch," begged Jock. But the gardener wouldn't.

"No," he said. "I'm not going to be by my bonfire all day, and I can't keep an eye on you to see that you don't burn yourself. You just keep right away. Go along now—don't come past the hedge. If I see you any nearer I'll go along and tell your mother."

Well, gardener meant what he said, so Jock went off, sulking. It was too bad. A bonfire was just about the most exciting thing that happened in a garden—and he wasn't even allowed to watch it!

The gardener went at four o'clock that day. It wasn't quite Jock's tea-time, so he ran past the hedge and went right up to the bonfire. The horrid old gardener wasn't there to tell tales of him.

The bonfire was lovely. It flared up, as bright as could be. Jock stood near to it, feeling the warmth. Then the fire died down, and Jock looked round for something to put on it. Really, he was very naughty and disobedient, wasn't he?

He saw some leaves blowing in the wind. He gathered up a big handful and threw them on the fire. They caught in the flames and flared up beautifully.

"Lovely bonfire, splendid bonfire!" said Jock. "I do like you! You're all alive and glowing, and I like your yellow tongues of flame!"

The fire flared up as if it was glad to hear Jock praising it. A piece of half-burnt wood fell out. Jock picked it up. It was hot, and he dropped it quickly. He looked at his hand. It was sooty-black from the half-burnt stick.

"I'd better wipe the black off, or Mummy will ask me what I've been doing," he said. So he put his hand in his pocket to get out his handkerchief. He pulled it out to rub his hand clean, and, as he pulled it out, something else came with it—his paper money!

The wind saw it and pounced on it with glee. It blew it straight into the bonfire!

A little yellow flame reached out to it and licked the paper money. It flared up—burnt itself to a black, curly fragment—and dropped to bits.

"Oh! Oh! My five shillings!" cried Jock, in horror. "My new aeroplane! I shan't get it now! Oh! You horid bonfire! You, nasty, greedy, unkind bonfire! How I hate you!"

The silly boy kicked at it, and a shower of sparks flew out. One burnt his leg, and he fled down the garden, howling loudly.

"My paper money has gone! I can't buy my aeroplane!"

Mummy came rushing out to see what the

matter was. Jock flung himself into her arms. He poured out all the story, expecting to be comforted. Perhaps Mummy would give him five shillings now that his paper money was burnt.

But Mummy didn't even smile. She looked rather solemn and sad. "I'm sorry about your paper money," she said. "But I am much, much sorrier to know I have such a silly, disobedient little boy. I think it was a very good punishment for you, Jock. If you think about it a little, you will see that you deserved to lose your money. I told you to put it into your purse, and you didn't. I told you not to go near the bonfire, and you did. Well, I've told you before, you can't do wrong things without something horrid happening to you. It's no use crying. You made this happen yourself. You must be brave about it, and just make up your mind not to grumble or whine, because, after all, it was nobody's fault but yours!"

Jock dried his eyes. He was quite hurt because his mother didn't pet him and comfort him. He told the gardener all about the burning of his paper money the next day, and the gardener didn't seem a bit sorry either.

"Serves you right!" he said. "Now keep away from me to-day, please. I've no time for naughty

little boys. You may go and do something worse
to-day for all I know."

"I shan't," said Jock, in rather a small voice.
"I've been very unhappy about losing the aeroplane that my money was going to buy—and
nobody has been nice to me about it, just when I
wanted them to be nice. So to-day I'm going to be
nice to everyone, instead of disobedient—and then
perhaps people will be nice to *me*."

"I shouldn't be surprised," said the gardener.
"Well—if you are still feeling like that this afternoon you can come and help me to tidy out the
shed—but only if you are *really* feeling good!"

I wonder if Jock will help the gardener this
afternoon. I rather think he will. Wasn't it a pity
that he lost his money like that?

THE WHIPPING-TOP

THERE WAS once a little wooden top that didn't like to be whipped. It was green, and had one strong steel leg on which it spun round and round very fast indeed.

It belonged to Jim. He had a whip, and with this whip he could make the top spin till it was quite giddy. All the toys used to watch the top spinning, and they would laugh and tease him.

"You must be very naughty, Top, to have to be whipped every day!" they said.

"I'm not naughty," the top said, crossly. "I am

very good. Jim only whips me to make me spin."

One day, when Jim was making his top spin on the pavement, he hit it so hard with the string of his whip that the top leapt high in the air. It came down again, spinning very fast, and it spun off down the road at a great pace. Jim was just going after it when he saw the fire-engine coming, and he forgot all about his top. The top was pleased.

"Now I shall run away from Jim," it thought. "I won't be whipped any more. I'll go on a fine adventure and never come back again."

So off he went, spinning fast down the road. A little dog saw him and stared in surprise.

"What are you?" asked the dog. "Come here and talk to me."

"Not I!" said the top, spinning away. "I've more important things to do!"

But the dog was so surprised to see such a queer spinning creature that he followed him. Soon the top met a rat, popping its head out of a drain.

"Are you good to eat?" called the rat. "Come over here and talk to me."

"Not I!" said the top. "I've more important things to do!" And he spun away fast. But the rat followed him, running a little way behind the dog.

Soon they met a prickly hedgehog, and he stared in astonishment. "You make me giddy to look at you," he said. "Come over here and talk to me."

"Not I!" said the top. "I've more important things to do." And off he spun again, feeling really very fine and grand.

"What important things is he going to do?" the hedgehog asked the dog and the rat. But they didn't know. So the hedgehog followed, too.

After a bit the top passed a cat sitting in the sun on the top of a wall. The cat looked down in surprise.

"Stop a bit!" she mewed. "Come and talk to me."

"Not I!" said the top, spinning faster than ever. "I've more important things to do."

"Well, if they are so important that a dog, a rat, and a hedgehog are following you, I shall come too," said the cat, and down she jumped. So there were four creatures all following the top, and didn't he feel important!

He skipped along and spun fast. He hummed a small song, and felt as happy as could be. He didn't look where he was going—and he bumped hard into the kerb. He fell over. He shook a little —and then lay quite still.

All the creatures came round him, though the rat kept an eye on the dog and the cat.

"He's gone to sleep," said the dog.

"He's dead," said the cat.

"He wasn't going to do anything important after all," said the hedgehog.

The top tried to spin itself, but it couldn't. All its spin was gone. It lay there by the kerb, quite still and very sad.

"I thought I could go spinning on for ever," it thought. "But I can't. I can't spin unless I am whipped. If I want any fun I'll have to get Jim to come along with his whip. Why did I make a fuss about it? All whipping-tops are whipped. Now I shall have to lie here all my life long and never spin again. And, oh, it was such fun to spin round and round on my one little leg!"

The rat ran off. The hedgehog shuffled away. The cat jumped to the top of the wall. Only the little dog was left. The top spoke to him.

"Little dog, do you know a boy called Jim? I do wish I could go back to him. But all my spin is gone, and I can't move."

"Yes—I know Jim," said the dog. "I'll take you back to him in my mouth, if you like."

And with that the kind little dog picked up the top in his mouth and ran up the hill with him. He found Jim and laid the top down at his feet.

"You clever little dog!" cried Jim, pleased. "I

thought my top was quite lost! Here is a biscuit for you. Now, Top, where have you been? You deserve a good whipping for running away!"

"A good whipping is just what I want!" cried the top, joyfully. "I shall spin again then!"

And you should just have seen it spin! Really, it spun round so fast that Jim could hardly see it. You may be sure it didn't run away again!

MIGGLE AND MISTER STAMP-ABOUT

THERE WAS once a funny little fellow called
Miggle. He was a kindly creature, always ready
with a joke and a smile, but he really was very
stupid.

Everyone teased him. Everyone said he had no
brains at all—which was perfectly true. They
just treated Miggle as a Great Big Joke.

And that made Miggle rather sad. He didn't
want to be just a Joke. He didn't want always to be
laughed at. He badly wanted to feel grown-up

and important, just sometimes. But nobody would let him.

One day Mister Stamp-About came to live in Miggle's village. He was a very bad-tempered fellow. He roared and shouted at everyone; he stamped about and made such a noise that the peaceful villagers were dreadfully scared.

"I wish he'd go away," said Jinky.

"I wish he'd never come," said Feefo.

"Let's tell him we don't want him in our village," said Tiptoe.

So they told him. But Mister Stamp-About went purple in the face, and stamped so hard that he made a thick dust that choked everyone and made them cough.

"What! You dare to tell me what to do!" yelled Mister Stamp-About, his hair standing straight on end. "Just wait till I catch one of you, that's all! I'll slap him till he's nothing but a trembling jelly!"

Now everyone knew quite well that Mister Stamp-About would certainly keep his word, so they all fled away at once. Nobody wanted to meet Stamp-About any more. Everyone went another way when they saw him.

And, as you can guess, poor little Miggle was more afraid than anyone. He just shivered in his shoes when he even heard Stamp-About's voice in the distance. For one thing, Miggle had once laughed loudly at Stamp-About when the wind had blown his hat off, and Stamp-About had never forgiven him for that.

"I know he would pull every hair out of my head, and swing me round by my nose or ears, and do something dreadful to me if he caught me," thought poor Miggle. So he didn't go near Stamp-About if he could possibly help it.

He was very glad when Feefo asked him to go over the hill to the next village to fetch him a barrel of apples.

"You may be a silly fellow, Miggle, but you're strong," said Feefo. "So go over to my aunt's, and ask her to give you a barrel of red apples for me. Carry it back to me and I'll give you sixpence."

"Right!" said Miggle, and set off. He got the barrel of apples, set it on his shoulder, and climbed to the top of the hill over which he had to go to get back to his own village.

And, oh dear me, goodness gracious, who should be coming up the hill-path but Mister Stamp-About himself! Miggle knew he hadn't time to turn and go back down the hill, and he simply couldn't face Stamp-About. He didn't know what to do.

Then he had an idea. Stamp-About hadn't yet seen him. Miggle would empty out the apples and get inside the barrel. He could hide there well. Maybe Stamp-About would go right past him and not notice the barrel at all.

So, in a great hurry, Miggle emptied out the apples and got inside the barrel. It stood there on the hill top, quite still.

But the apples rolled and bumped merrily down the hill! You should have seen them! They shot down the path and bumped into Stamp-About. He was most surprised. He thought someone was throwing them at him, and he was very angry. He began to shout.

"How dare you throw apples at me! How dare you! Wait till I get you! Oh, you'll be sorry for yourself then, you certainly will!"

Now Miggle heard all this, and he began to shake like a jelly. He shook so hard that he jerked the barrel over on its side. And, of course, the barrel began to roll down the hill! Down it went and down, going faster and faster as it rolled. It leapt over stones, and made a tremendous noise— clitter, clatter, bang, crash, bump, clatter!

Miggle was being turned over and over inside as the barrel shot down the hill. He felt terribly giddy and very frightened, but he just couldn't do anything about it.

Stamp-About heard the noise, and looked to see what it was. When he saw the big barrel coming jumping down the hill-path he was really scared. He turned to run.

Down the path he went, with the barrel after him, singing clitter, clatter, bang, crash, bump, clatter!

"It's chasing me, it's chasing me!" cried Stamp-About, in a dreadful fright. "Stop it, somebody, stop it!"

The little folk of the village had come out to watch. They laughed till their sides ached when they saw what was happening. As for stopping

the barrel, well, no one was going to do that! No—let it catch Stamp-About if it could!

Stamp-About got to the bottom of the hill, panting and shouting. The barrel got there, too, rolling very fast indeed. It bumped over a tree-root, sprang high into the air, and landed right on top of Stamp-About! He went down, bump, just like a skittle.

"It's caught me, it's caught me!" he yelled. "Oh, save me, save me!"

But nobody saved him. The barrel rolled a little way off, and then stayed still.

Stamp-About got up. He was covered with bruises. He looked in fright at the barrel.

"Run, Stamp-About, before it chases you again!" cried the little folk. And Stamp-About ran. How he ran! He ran and he ran—and he never came back. He was gone for ever.

And then, after a while, poor, bruised, giddy Miggle stuck his head up out of the barrel. Everyone stared at him in the very greatest astonishment. Miggle looked at Feefo. He was very much afraid that Feefo would scold him for losing all his apples.

But nobody scolded him at all! To Miggle's enormous surprise they all crowded round him and patted him wherever they could reach him.

"Miggle! You clever fellow! So it was you who thought of that marvellous idea!" they cried. "Why, Miggle, you are Simply Wonderful!"

"No, I'm not," said Miggle. "You see—I was afraid—and I . . ."

79

But nobody would let him explain. They all thought he had done a really marvellous thing, and was a great hero. So Miggle began to smile and feel very happy indeed.

And now at last Miggle is no longer treated as a Joke. He is Somebody! People listen to him, and tell him he is a grand fellow. Well, well—it may have been an accident that he chased Stamp-About away, but it did old Miggle a lot of good, didn't it!

TIMOTHY'S TADPOLES

TIMOTHY WAS rather like you—he loved kittens and puppies, little chicks and skippetty lambs. He loved visiting the farm to see the horses and cows, he loved going by the river to watch the swans sail by, and he always enjoyed going to the pond to catch the wriggling black tadpoles in the spring-time.

But this year Timothy wouldn't go to the pond with the others. He didn't want to catch tadpoles.

"But why not?" said his mother. "Dick is going, and Joan. Why don't you take your net and go, too?"

"Well, Mother," said Timothy, "I've caught little black tadpoles for three years now—and our teacher at school says they turn into frogs. But they don't. They just die! And I don't want that to happen to them again this year. What's the use of my going to the pond and fishing those funny little tadpoles out of their home, and putting them in a jam-jar, and then bringing them home to die?"

"Well, Timothy, just no use at all," said his mother, surprised. "They ought to turn into frogs, not die. There must be something wrong about the way you keep them when you bring them home."

"I wish my Uncle Fred was coming to stay," said Timothy. "He knows all about things like that. I wouldn't mind going tadpoling with him. I'm sure *his* tadpoles would grow into frogs!"

Well, Timothy got a surprise on Saturday morning—for who should turn up but his favourite Uncle Fred! He shouted to Timothy, and the little boy ran to greet him.

"Timothy! It's a marvellous day—what about going tadpoling?" said Uncle Fred.

Mother laughed when she heard that. "Tim won't go tadpoling this year," she said. "He says that he's not going to bring tadpoles home to die. He only wants them if they will live and show him how they change into little frogs."

"Quite right, too," said Uncle Fred. "I wouldn't

dream of bringing home anything that was going to die. I wouldn't be so cruel. No, Timothy— we'll go and get some tadpoles that will live happily at home with you, and show you exactly how they change into frogs."

"Well, all the other children's tadpoles die, too," said Timothy. "It's horrid. Hardly any of them live to change into frogs."

"Get your net and a glass jam-jar and we'll go right away," said Uncle Fred. Mother quickly cut some sandwiches for them, and off they went.

It was a lovely walk to the pond. Uncle Fred

knew all about birds and animals, flowers and trees, so he was a lovely person to go out with. When they came to the pond they looked into the water.

"Stickle-backs—and hundreds and hundreds of tadpoles, little black wrigglers," said Timothy, excited. "And water-snails. Look at them! I can easily catch the tadpoles."

He caught dozens and put them into the jam-jar. But Uncle Fred soon shook his head.

"Here's your first mistake," he said. "Look— you've put about sixty tadpoles into one small jar, Tim. There isn't enough air in that water for more than six to breathe. You will have to empty out all of them except five or six."

"Really?" said Timothy surprised. But he did as he was told. He tipped up the jar, and almost all of the black tadpoles dripped back into the pond. Only six were left.

"Now we'll put a few water-snails in with them," said Uncle Fred.

"Why?" asked Timothy.

"Well, because the snails eat all the rubbish in the water and keep it pure and clean," said Uncle Fred. "They are the dustmen of the pond, you know. So we will put four or five into our jar."

In they went. Then Uncle Fred made Timothy

pull up a little bright green water-weed for the jar.

"We'll make the jar as like a little pond as we can," he said. "Tadpoles like the water-weed in the pond—so they shall have some in their jar. There—doesn't it look nice, Timothy?"

It did. Timothy was pleased. "I'd like to take the jar home and show Mother the tadpoles, water-weed, and all the snails," he said. "Let's have our sandwiches and then go home."

So they ate their lunch, and watched the little black moor-hens that swam across the pond, bobbing their heads to and fro like clockwork. Then they went home. Timothy carried the jar very carefully.

They met some other children, who also had jam-jars full of tadpoles.

"Is that all the tadpoles you could find, Tim?" they cried. "Look at ours! We've got hundreds."

"That's too many for your small jars," said Timothy. "Yours will die. Mine won't."

When he got home Timothy showed his mother the jar of tadpoles and snails. She thought it looked very nice. "Now go and put it in the nursery," she said. So off went Tim. He chose a very sunny window-sill and put the jar of tadpoles there, right in the golden sunshine.

Uncle Fred came in. He stared at the jar. "I say, Tim!" he said, "do you want to cook your poor tadpoles? The sun will make that water so warm that they will be almost cooked in half-an-hour's time!"

"I thought they liked the sun," said Timothy.

"So they do—but not when they are in a small jar instead of a big, cool pond where there are all sorts of places they can hide in if they get too hot," said his Uncle. "My word, Tim—no wonder your poor tadpoles die every year if you cook them in the sun."

"I think I've been rather silly before," said Timothy, going red. "I've overcrowded the poor things in a small jar—and cooked them in the sun, too. No wonder they died. Do you think they would like to be on the other window-sill, Uncle, where it's warm but not in the sun?"

"Yes," said his Uncle. So the jar of tadpoles went there.

"What do I feed them on?" asked Timothy. "I usually put bread in."

"Yes—and it goes all bad and sour in the water!" said Uncle Fred. "No—no bread, Tim. If you want to feed them properly it's best to go to the pond each day and bring back a tin of pond-water. There is lots of insect-life in the water that the growing tadpoles feed on. But if the pond is too far you must get a bit of raw meat from Mother, tie it to a thread, and let it hang in the water for a while. The tadpoles will come to feed on it, and when they have had enough you can pull the meat out by the thread. It won't go bad then, and make the water bad, too."

So sometimes Timothy gave his tadpoles a tiny bit of meat tied to a thread, and sometimes he went to the pond and brought back a tin of water to add to the jar.

His tadpoles grew. How they grew! And one

morning Mother heard such squeals coming from the nursery that she really had to go and see what the matter was.

"My tadpoles have got back legs! They've got back legs!" cried Timothy. "Look! Look! Soon they'll have front legs, too, and then they will really begin to look like frogs!"

Well, they got their front legs, too. Then their long tails seemed to get shorter and shorter—and before long those tadpoles began to look much more like little frogs than like black tadpoles!

"Mother," said Timothy one day, "do you know, it's very sad—*all* those tadpoles that Dick and Joan caught have died. Every single one. And all mine are alive, and have turned into tiny frogs. To-day I put a bit of wood to float at the top of the jar, so that they could climb up on it and breathe the air there. Mother, soon I can let them free. They will live in our garden."

"Well, I hope they won't do any harm," said Mother.

"Uncle Fred says they will be friends to us," said Timothy. "They will eat caterpillars, grubs, and flies. Mother, won't it be fun to see little frogs working for us in our garden? Whenever I see them I shall think, ' Ha! You were once my little black tadpoles! '"

I've seen Timothy's little frogs. They are still very small, because it will take them five years to be grown-up frogs. But although they are small, what a lot of flies and grubs they eat! Ah, they are Timothy's friends all right!

And Timothy says: If *you* go to catch tadpoles, do what he did, please. Only put a few in a jar— keep them out of the sun—and feed them properly. Then you, too, will have the joy of seeing them turn into frogs, and work for you in your garden!

THE BIG BAD DOG

THERE WAS once a puppy who grew up into a very big dog. He was bigger than any other dog in the town—and, my goodness, what a fine time he had, to be sure!

He chased all the cats. He ran after all the little dogs, and when he found that he was growing bigger than even the big dogs he snapped at them, too, and barked loudly whenever they went by.

He was quite mad with joy to find that everything ran away from him. And then, one day, he barked at a little boy and frightened him.

The little boy began to cry. Jocko, the dog, was surprised to find that he could frighten even a boy. He ran after him, trying to pull at his coat. Of course, it was only in play, but the little boy was terribly afraid.

Well, after that Jocko tried jumping up at a little girl. She was so frightened that she dropped her doll and broke it. She ran home sobbing, and the big bad dog jumped round her, barking in delight. What fun to frighten everyone and make them run away from him like that!

He didn't really want to hurt anyone. He was just a bad, grown-up puppy who loved frightening animals and people. And because he was so big, no other cat, dog, or child dared to snap at him or smack him.

"I'm afraid of his big teeth," said the large black cat on the wall.

"I'm afraid he might snap at my ears," said the little white dog.

"I'm afraid that big dog will bite me," said the boys and girls on their way to school.

Well, after a while Jocko tried barking madly at women going to market. They were frightened, too. Then he tried barking at motor-cycles and motor-cars. Really, he had great fun, but how everybody hated him.

Jocko belonged to an old lady who couldn't manage him at all. She tried locking him up, but he jumped out of the window. She tried smacking him, but he didn't mind that a scrap. She tried scolding him, but Jocko just jumped up and put his big paws on her shoulders to lick her cheek— and he nearly knocked her over!

"I'm sure I don't know what in the world to do with you!" sighed the old lady. "One of these days you really will get into trouble."

Now one day a circus came to the town. All round the walls were pasted big posters. "Mr. Galliano's Circus is here! Come and see Lotta and her lovely horse, Black Beauty! Come and see Jimmy and his marvellous dog, Lucky! Jumbo is here, and Lilliput with his Monkeys!"

Now just about that time Jocko was really and truly at his very worst. He had barked at the baker's boy and made him drop buns and loaves all over the road. He had leapt up at the postman and torn a bit out of his sleeve—and he had frightened a little girl so much that she wouldn't go to school.

All the dogs in the town met together about it.

"We'll just *have* to do something about Jocko," said Spot.

"He's getting worse and worse," said Rover.

"He's so big, that's the worst of it," said Tinker.

"None of us can stop him because he is bigger than any of us."

"Oh, if only we could find a bigger dog than he is, and ask it to give him a fright!" said Patch.

Now just then Spot caught sight of a big poster-picture of the circus, pasted on a fence nearby. On it was a picture of old Jumbo, the elephant. Spot scratched himself and thought hard.

"I suppose it wouldn't be any use asking Jumbo, that big elephant, to help us?" he said. "If only we could get *him* to chase Jocko, maybe he'd have such a fright that he'd never frighten other animals and children again."

"Well, I know Lucky, Jimmy's circus dog," said Rover, his plumy tail wagging hard. "I could go and ask him to get Jumbo to do that! I'll go now."

And off he went. He explained to Lucky exactly what Jocko was doing, and how everyone wanted him to get a real fright to stop him being such a bad dog. Lucky listened hard.

"Oh yes, that can easily be managed," he said. "I will tell old Jumbo all you've said. Now listen, Rover; you get Jocko in a field or yard somewhere —where he can't get out—and I'll bring old Jumbo there to-morrow. Then we'll see what happens! It should be very funny!"

Rover rushed back to the other dogs. They all wagged their tails in delight. "How can we get Jocko into a field or yard?" asked Patch.

"Easy!" said Tinker. "I'll take one of my bones to the old brick-yard behind the police-station. If the gate is shut no one can get out. I'll run in with my bone—and you, Patch, tell Jocko that I've gone there, and he'll come after me to get the bone. Then I'll run away as if I were frightened, and we'll shut the gate. We'll keep Jocko there, gnawing my bone, till Lucky brings along Jumbo. Then we'll open the gate and let Jumbo in!"

All the dogs were most excited about their plan. The cats soon got to hear of it, too, and the next day there were about thirty cats sitting on the high wall that ran round the brick-yard, waiting to see what was going to happen.

It was easy to get Jocko into the yard. Patch told him that Tinker had a fine bone, and Jocko at once ran off to frighten Tinker and get his bone. Tinker pretended to be very much afraid, and ran into the brick-yard. Jocko ran after him. Tinker dropped his bone and tore out of the gate, his tail between his legs.

"Silly dog!" barked Jocko, beginning to crunch the bone. He didn't hear the click as the gate of the yard shut. He just went on joyfully gnawing the big bone.

Soon Lucky came along with Jumbo, the enormous grey elephant. He was really a gentle and kind creature, but to-day he meant to be angry and fierce.

"I am very large indeed," he said to the dogs

with him. "But I do not use my strength to frighten or hurt others. No one should ever do that. The bigger and the more powerful anyone is, the kinder and more gentle they should be. It is wicked to use power and strength to hurt others smaller or weaker than ourselves. We elephants never do that."

"Well, just teach Jocko that lesson!" said Patch. "He's the biggest dog in the town—and the worst!"

Patch pushed open the gate of the brick-yard. Jumbo went in. The gate clicked shut. Jocko looked up from his bone, expecting to see Tinker back again.

But there stood an enormous animal, higher than the wall—as high as a small house!

Jocko dropped his bone. His tail went between his legs. He had never seen an elephant in his life before, and he hadn't even known such a big animal lived on the earth. He simply couldn't believe his eyes!

Jumbo lifted up his trunk and made a loud trumpeting sound, "Hr-r-r-r-rumph! Hr-r-r-r-rumph!" Jocko began to tremble. He squashed himself into a corner, and hoped that the big animal wouldn't see him.

Jumbo went towards him on his big, clumsy

legs. They seemed like tree-trunks to poor Jocko. Jumbo trumpeted again. Jocko ran out of his corner, full of fear. Jumbo ran after him.

All the cats on the wall laughed till they nearly fell off. The dogs watching through the gate wagged their tails joyfully. At last, big, bad Jocko was getting a little bit of what he had given to so many others. And he wasn't liking it at all!

"Don't chase me, don't chase me!" he barked.

"But you chase others!" trumpeted Jumbo.

"Don't bite me, you're so big!" yelped Jocko.

"But you bite and snap at others, though they beg you not to, because, to them, *you* are big!" trumpeted the elephant.

Jocko ran under a pile of bricks and crouched there. Jumbo saw a big tank full of water nearby.

He put in his trunk and sucked up the water.

Then he put it down towards Jocko and squirted him all over with the cold water! The dog was so frightened that he darted out of the hiding-place, yelping with fear.

"How do you like being chased?" cried the watching cats.

"How do you like being frightened?" barked the excited dogs.

"How do you like someone bigger than you are trying to hurt you?" yelped Patch.

"Mind he doesn't eat you!" yapped Spot.

"Save me, save me!" barked poor Jocko, running round and round the yard, with Jumbo lumbering after him. "I'll never chase anyone again! I'll never frighten anyone! I didn't know it felt like this. Oh, how sorry I am I ever gave any of you a fright!"

"We'll pretend to rescue him, and then we'll make him keep his promise," said Rover. So the dogs pushed open the gate and tore in, pretending to rescue Jocko. Jumbo went off with little dog Lucky, trumpeting to himself whenever he thought of big bad Jocko getting such a fright.

"He's gone—that big creature has gone!" said Rover to Jocko. "He came and gave you a fright because he had heard that that was the sort of thing *you* did to others! Now see you never do it again, Jocko. You should know that the bigger you are, the kinder you should be!"

"Oh, I will be," groaned Jocko, lying down because he was so tired after all his chasing. "I tell you I didn't know what it felt like to be frightened and chased. Nobody has ever done it to me before. I'm not really bad. I just didn't know. I'm going to be kind now, I really am."

"Well, mind you are," said Patch, "or I'm sure that great elephant will be along here again to teach you a lesson!"

Jocko ran off to his mistress. He met a small dog with a bone on the way, but he took no notice. He saw a cat, but he didn't chase her. He met two little children, and he didn't even bark at them. So maybe he has learnt his lesson after all. And didn't Jimmy laugh when little dog Lucky told him the story!

BILLY'S BICYCLE

BILLY HAD a bicycle. It had belonged to his brother, and when John had grown too big for it he had put it into the shed and left it there all by itself. John had had a new one, and so the old bicycle had lain there, rusty and forgotten.

When Billy grew big enough for a bicycle he remembered John's. "Oh, I wonder if it would do for me, or if it is too broken and old!" he thought.

So he went to have a look at it. There it was in the shed, leaning against the seed-boxes and the barrel of oil.

Billy looked at it. "I like the look of you," he said to the bicycle. "You certainly look old, but you look nice and friendly somehow—as if you'd like me to ride on you."

Now this was just exactly what the bicycle *was* feeling! It badly wanted Billy to ride it. It liked the look of him very much, for Billy was one of those smiley children that everyone likes.

Billy took the bicycle out into the garden. "My goodness, you *are* rusty!" he said. "And your paint is all worn off. Your bell is broken— it won't ring—and your basket is falling to pieces. I don't think much of you at the moment, but I do believe I could make you quite grand again if I get a pot of paint and if I rub the rust off your bright parts."

The bicycle was thrilled to hear this. It is dreadful to be old, rusty, and dirty—and simply lovely to hear somebody say that they can make you look fine again. The bicycle wished it had a bell to ring. It felt quite sure it would have rung it for joy if it had!

Well, Billy was as good as his word. He spent some money on a pot of black paint and a pot of red paint. He painted that bicycle till it looked as new and gay as could be. He rubbed away the rust and made the bright parts shine.

"I'll buy a new bell for you and a new basket," said Billy. "I'll have your brakes put right, too. And there's a screw gone at the back. I'll get that put right. And I'll pump up your tyres and ride you! What ho! You and I will have some fine times together, bike!"

Well, in a week's time that bicycle was really just like a new one. It shone beautifully, and its new bell rang as loudly as could be! Its tyres were nice and hard, and spun along the road joyfully.

The old bicycle was very happy. It loved to feel Billy on its saddle, pedalling away hard. It helped him all it could. It tried not to run over big stones. It tried not to go into puddles and splash him.

They had some fine times together, Billy and the bike. They went everywhere—to school, to the park, to the hills, and to the woods. The bicycle enjoyed itself tremendously. It had been so lonely and sad lying in the dark shed by itself.

Now it could talk to other bicycles and cars, and it had its bell rung at corners, so that it felt most important! Ah, this was the kind of life for a bicycle!

Billy kept his bicycle beautifully. He cleaned it well. He kept the bright parts shining. He oiled it and pumped up the tyres properly. He didn't fling it down on the ground as other boys did with their bicycles. And the old bike loved him for it, and sang a little purring song as it went along the road.

"I wish I could do something for Billy!" it sang. "Billy's done plenty for me! I wish I could do something for Billy! Billy's done plenty for me!"

Now one evening, when the bicycle was leaning against the shed, waiting for Billy to come out and put it away, it was surprised to see a boy's head peeping just over the fence.

"What's that boy doing?" thought the bicycle, in surprise. "Why is he peeping all round like that? This is very strange."

The boy saw that nobody was about. He jumped over the fence and ran to the apple-shed, in which were stored all the cooking and eating apples. My word, that boy was going to have a feast!

The bicycle watched him go into the apple-shed. He heard him munching apples. He saw him filling a sack with them. And the bicycle was very angry!

"Billy's mother may think that Billy took those apples!" it said.

It wondered what to do. It couldn't ride off by itself and warn Billy. But it could ring its bell!

So it rang it. "R-r-r-ring, r-r-r-ring, r-r-r-ring! R-r-r-ring!"

The boy in the shed was alarmed. He put his head out to see what was happening. He didn't for one moment think that it was the bicycle bell ringing!

But he saw the bicycle, and an idea came into his head. He could ride it away quickly and nobody would catch him!

He put the sack of apples over his shoulder, ran

to the bicycle, jumped on it, and rode away. The bicycle rang its bell in despair.

"R-r-r-ring! R-r-r-ring! R-r-r-ring!"

But Billy was out with his father and couldn't hear it. So out of the gate the bike had to go, with the bad boy riding it. How it hated it! But it couldn't help itself, for when its pedals were pushed round and round it just had to go!

And then, coming down the street, the bicycle saw Billy and his father! They were going home. The bicycle was so excited. Now perhaps Billy would see it!

But Billy was looking into the shops as he passed and he didn't notice his bicycle. So the bicycle rang its bell desperately again: "R-r-r-ring! R-r-r-ring! R-r-r-ring!"

Billy looked round. He knew the sound of that

bicycle bell. He stared hard at the bicycle as it went by. Could it possibly be his? No—surely it couldn't!

The bicycle saw a big stone in its way. It ran at it, and wobbled over it. The bad boy tried to balance himself, but he couldn't because the bicycle wobbled so. Down he fell with a crash—and the apples flew all over the road!

Billy and his father went to help him up. The bicycle rang its bell again. "R-r-r-ring! R-r-r-ring! R-r-r-ring!"

Then Billy looked closely at the bicycle, and he knew that it was his. What an extraordinary thing!

"What are you doing on my bicycle?" he asked the boy, sternly. "You bad boy—and I believe those are our apples, too!"

The boy began to cry. He had hurt his knee very badly, and he was frightened, for he knew that he had done very wrong. He confessed all that he had done, and Billy's father looked very stern.

"You will come back to our house and I will bind up your knee," he said. "Then I shall take you back to your own home and speak to your father about you. I think you need to have a good punishment, and I shall see that you get it.

How dare you come to my apple-shed, steal my apples. and ride off on my son's bicycle! It's a good thing you rang the bell when you did, or Billy wouldn't have heard it and looked round."

"I *didn't* ring the bell," said the boy, wiping his eyes with a very dirty hand. "It seemed to ring all by itself. It was very queer."

"Bells don't ring by themselves," said Billy's father. But he was wrong, wasn't he? And, just to show that he was, the bicycle rang its bell again, very softly and happily:

"R-r-r-ring! R-r-r-ring! R-r-r-ring! I've done something for Billy at last! R-r-r-ring! R-r-r-ring! R-r-r-ring!"

THE LITTLE RACEHORSES

ONCE UPON a time Linda and George had a race-horse game given to them for Christmas. It was a lovely game, and the horses were fine. There were four of them—one black, one brown, one white, and one grey. Their legs were stretched out just as if they were running a real race.

They ran on a board, and Linda and George threw dice to see how far to move them along. Sometimes Linda's horse won, and sometimes George's did.

"I wish they could *really* race," said Linda. "Wouldn't it be fun to see them tearing round the nursery, George?"

But they didn't tear round the nursery. When they were not on the race-board they were in the box, quiet and still.

One afternoon, when Linda and George were out for a walk, a strange thing happened in the nursery. The excitement began outside the window first, and all the toys wondered whatever could be happening.

The golliwog climbed up on the window-sill to see. He called to the others.

"I say! A horrid little gnome has got hold of one of the little elves who live in the Michaelmas daisies! He's taking her away! All the elves will be after him in a minute! Oh, my goodness me!"

"What's happened now?" asked the teddy-bear, trying to climb up to see.

"Why, the gnome has got one of the field-mice to ride!" cried the gollywog. "My word, he's off! —and he's taken the little elf with him. Hear her squeal, poor thing!"

The toys heard her squealing, and they were very sorry. Then the golliwog gave a yell. "Here come all the elves to rescue their friend. Too late, too late! The gnome has gone off on the mouse. And that mouse can run very fast indeed!"

Suddenly there was a fluttering of silvery wings, and into the nursery flew a crowd of small and anxious elves. They called to the toys: "Please, please help us! Where's the clockwork train? We want to chase the wicked gnome in it."

"It's broken," said the teddy-bear, sadly. "George trod on the engine by mistake."

"Well, where's the clockwork motor-car then?" cried an elf, looking all round.

"The key is lost," said the golliwog. "So that's no use, either."

"What about the toy aeroplane?" cried another elf.

"George has given it away," said the bear. "Oh dear, whatever can we do to help you?"

Then there came a noise from the racehorse box. The little horses were trying to lift the lid with their heads. The golliwog ran to take it off. The four horses leapt out at once.

"Let *us* take you to chase the wicked gnome!" they cried. "We are racehorses. We are used to racing. We can go as fast as the wind!"

"Oh, fine!" cried the elves, and two of them flew to sit on the backs of each horse.

"Off you go!" cried the elves on the brown horse—and off it went. You should have seen it!

It tore out of the nursery door on its four noisy little feet and rushed down the passage to the garden. After it galloped all the other little race-horses—and what a noise they made!

Clippitty clop, clippitty clop, clippitty clop! Their hooves clattered down the passage. The garden door was just a bit open, and they went through the crack in a trice, with the elves holding on for all they were worth.

Out into the garden they went, and down the path. Clippitty clop, clippitty clop! The elves yelled and bounced up and down on the horses' backs. They were really enjoying themselves.

"Run, horses, run!" they shouted, and smacked the good little horses on the back with their small hands. "You'll soon catch up the gnome on the field-mouse!"

Well, after a while the elves saw the gnome in the distance, and they shouted for joy. "We are gaining on him!" they cried. "Run, horses, run!"

Clippitty clop, clippitty clop, on went the horses as fast as ever they could. This was fine! This was much, much better than going round the race-board!

They slowly overtook the field-mouse. The gnome suddenly heard the sound of the horses' hoofs and turned round to see what the noise was. When he saw the galloping horses with the elves on their backs he was frightened. He clutched the little elf more tightly, and hit the field-mouse hard.

"Quick, quick!" he cried. "They are after us!"

The mouse ran as fast as he could, but he was getting tired. After all, he was only a mouse, and not a racehorse. So he ran more and more slowly, and the gnome got very angry. He smacked the mouse so hard that it squealed.

Then it stopped and spoke angrily. "I am not going to be smacked like that when I am doing my best. I won't run a step further!"

And he wouldn't, no matter how hard the gnome begged him! So in a minute or two the mouse and the gnome were surrounded by the little racehorses, and there they were, prisoners in the middle. The elves leapt off their horses and ran to catch the gnome. They set free their little friend, and she ran to pat the racehorses, who were panting for breath.

The elves tied the gnome on the field-mouse and led them both away. But before they went they thanked the little horses a thousand times for their kindness.

"We couldn't possibly have caught the gnome

without you," they said. "How very, very fast
you run! You are certainly the fastest racehorses in the world!"

"Do you really think so?" asked the little
horses, pleased. "Oh, we *are* glad!"

"Can you find the way home by yourselves?"
asked the elves.

"Of course," said the horses. "Good-bye. We
will see you again another day."

Off they galloped, very proud and pleased.
They came at last to their own garden, and
galloped up the path. Clippitty clop, clippitty
clop, went their feet.

Now Linda and George were just coming in
from their walk when they heard the noise of the
little racehorses coming up the path—and, lo
and behold, four tiny horses galloped past them
at great speed and disappeared in at the garden
door!

"Linda! Did you see what I saw?" cried George,
in amazement.

"I saw what I thought were the horses from
our race-game!" cried Linda. "They were galloping! They really were! They looked as if they
had been out racing. Oh, George, we must be
dreaming!" So they went to the nursery and
looked. And there in the box were the four

horses, still panting a little, but lying quite still and quiet.

"They've got a little mud on their heels," said George, excited. "It *was* true, Linda. They really did pass us, and they must have been racing. Well, really, would you believe it?"

THE ONE-LEGGED MONKEY

JIMMY HAD a toy-monkey with long, swingy legs and a fine tail. He had a nice monkey-face with a smile, and Jimmy loved him with all his heart. He took him to bed with him at night because Monkey was so soft and cuddly.

One day he took Monkey out for a walk. He held Monkey by the hand and jerked him along as if he were walking. Monkey didn't like it very much because he felt sure that one of his legs was coming loose. The puppy had been in the nursery that morning, and had tugged at one of his legs—and now it didn't feel a bit nice.

Monkey looked down at his leg. Good gracious! It was almost off! It was hanging by a thread, and if Jimmy jerked him much more it would come off and be lost!

But he couldn't make Jimmy stop—and, oh dear, the next time that poor Monkey looked down he only had one leg. He was terribly upset.

"What will all the toys say? What will Jimmy say when he sees I've lost a leg? I'll not be able to walk or run at night any more, when all the toys come alive! Oh my, oh my, whatever shall I do?"

Jimmy didn't notice that Monkey had lost a leg until they were home. Then he suddenly saw, and he stared at Monkey in horror.

"You've only got one leg! Oh, you do look dreadful! Oh, I don't think I like you with one leg, Monkey. You look queer!"

Poor old Monkey! He did feel upset. *He* couldn't help only having one leg. The other was somewhere in the lane; he didn't know where.

That night the toys looked at Monkey and felt very sorry for him. "You look quite different," said the golliwog.

"You look rather horrid," said the baby-doll.

"I'm not sure that I like you now," said the bear.

And worst of all, Jimmy didn't take Monkey to bed with him that night. Monkey felt so lonely and strange sitting on the shelf. He cried little tears down his furry nose. He couldn't get down from the shelf because he only had one leg.

The toys felt sorry for him. "Monkey, cheer up! I'll go and see if I can find your lost leg," said the bear. "It must be somewhere in the lane. Then the curly-haired doll can sew it on for you. I'll go now."

The bear went out of the door, and the golliwog went with him. They ran down the garden and into the lane. The moon was shining and they could see everything quite clearly.

"Here's his leg!" cried the bear. But it was only a little stick.

"Here it is!" cried the golliwog—but no, it was a bit of rope. How the two of them hunted and hunted! But it didn't seem a bit of good—that leg was nowhere to be found.

Soon they met a little mouse hurrying along. He stopped and stared at the two toys, for he was not used to meeting bears and golliwogs at night.

"What are you looking for?" he asked.

"A leg!" said the bear.

"A *leg*!" said the mouse, astonished. "Do you really mean a *leg*? What a strange thing to look for! Are you expecting one to grow on a tree or something, or sprout up from the ground?"

"Don't be silly," said the golliwog. "We are looking for the leg that belongs to the toy-monkey. He lost it along here this morning, poor thing."

"Oh—I believe I know where it is!" said the mouse. "I didn't know it was a leg—but now I come to think of it there was a foot on the end, so it must have been."

"Where is it? Quick, tell us!" cried the bear.

"Long-Ears the Rabbit found it and took it to his hole," said the mouse. He pointed with a tiny paw to a rabbit-hole nearby. "He lives down there. You'd better hurry, because he told me he was going to eat it."

"*Eat* it!" cried the golliwog in horror. "But surely rabbits don't eat things like that! Come, Bear, let's run."

Down the hole the two of them went. They soon came to Long-Ears. He was peacefully asleep, but he woke up as soon as he heard the pattering feet of the two toys. Just by him was the leg of the monkey! How pleased the bear and the golliwog were!

"We've come for that leg," said the bear.

"But I want it," said Long-Ears. "It's full of sawdust, and I like sawdust to eat. I found it—and finding is keeping isn't it?"

"Indeed it isn't!" said the bear at once. "Only dishonest people say that! It belongs to our poor toy-monkey, and he is dreadfully unhappy about it. He usually goes to bed with Jimmy, but Jimmy doesn't like him with only one leg, so he hasn't taken him to bed with him to-night. You simply can't think how sad Monkey is about that."

"Well, I suppose you must take the leg back," said the rabbit, sadly. "Can't you give me any-thing instead? What about a lettuce?"

"There aren't any yet," said the bear.

"Well, a carrot?" said the rabbit.

"Sometimes Jimmy has carrots in his stew for dinner," said the bear. "Nurse puts his plate of stew on the table to cool and then she goes to wash Jimmy's hands. Maybe I could jump up on Jimmy's chair and take a carrot from his plate for you. I'm sure he wouldn't mind if he knew it was to get back Monkey's leg."

"All right," said the rabbit. "Take the leg. It's a good thing I hadn't begun to eat it! I meant to have it for my breakfast to-morrow morning!"

The bear and the golliwog carried the leg between them. They were so pleased to have got it. When they came into the nursery with it the toys ran round them in excitement.

"You've got it, you've got it! How clever of you! Where was it?"

The bear told the whole story, and the toys listened in delight. "Well, I'm sure Jimmy wouldn't mind giving all his carrots and his turnips and onions, too, now that Monkey has got back his leg!" cried the curly-haired doll, running to Nurse's work-basket and taking out a needle and cotton.

"Come here, Monkey," she said, when she had

got everything ready. "I will sew your leg on as neatly as can be, and I won't hurt you a scrap."

"Oh, I don't mind if you do," said Monkey, bravely. And he didn't. He sat there as good as gold whilst the doll sewed his leg on as tightly as she could. She didn't want him to lose it again.

Well, you can just imagine how glad Monkey was when he could walk and run again! He tore round and round the nursery in delight, and knocked over the clockwork mouse.

"Sorry!" he said. "So sorry! But I can't help feeling happy all over me!"

Next morning Jimmy looked for Monkey, and when he saw him sitting on the shelf—with TWO legs—he stared and he stared.

"Why, Monkey, you lost a leg yesterday," he said. "Now you've got it back again. You look like my own dear Monkey once more. I shall take you to bed with me to-night—I *did* miss you last night!"

And he hugged Monkey so tightly that he could hardly breathe. But Monkey liked it.

That morning there was stew for lunch. Nurse put out Jimmy's on the table to cool, and then went to see that he washed his hands and brushed his hair properly. Quick as lightning the bear climbed up on Jimmy's chair and took the big red carrot off his plate. He hid it at the back of the brick-box, ready to take to Long-Ears the Rabbit that night.

And when Jimmy came back, how he stared at

his plate! "You didn't give me any carrot, Nurse," he said.

"Yes, I did," said Nurse. "You must have eaten it!"

"But I *didn't*!" said Jimmy, astonished. And he is still puzzled about that missing carrot. You can tell him where it went, if you like—but I'm not sure he will believe you!

THE ENCHANTED CLOAK

ONCE UPON a time the Princess Peronel asked
Thimble, the pixie, to make her a very special
cloak.

She came to see Thimble in the middle of the
night. It was very exciting for Thimble, who was
in bed and fast asleep. She had to get up and put
on her dressing-gown, and curtsey to the Princess
when she opened the door.

"Thimble, this is a secret," whispered the
Princess, looking all round to make sure there
was no one else there. "I want this cloak to wear

on Midsummer Night—and I have two very special spells that I want you to sew into it as you make it."

"What spells?" asked Thimble, going red with excitement.

"One is a spell that will make me know everything as soon as I put it on," said Peronel. "And the other is powerful magic that will grant my wishes. Here are the two spells—do be careful of them."

"It will be a very magic cloak," said Thimble. "What do you want me to make it of?"

"I want it made of the purple twilight," said the Princess. "That's difficult, I know—but maybe you can get some of the purple. Line it with some silver-dawn sky, will you? And sew the spells in all the time. Don't tell anyone, whatever you do!"

Thimble promised. She was very pleased to have such important work to do.

"You see, I want to wear the magic cloak on Midsummer Night, and be able to grant wishes to those pixies and fairies who deserve it," said the Princess. "I shall know everything as soon as I put on the cloak—so I shall know which pixies deserve to have wishes given to them and which don't. It will be marvellous."

She said good-bye and went. Thimble was so excited that she couldn't go to sleep any more that night. She took her sharpest scissors and flew up to the middle part of the eastern sky. She waited till dawn—and then she cut a silvery piece of the sky right out, folded it up, and flew down to earth again. Now she had the lining for the cloak! A cloud came to fill up the hole she had made.

She asked a brownie to get her some purple twilight, and he came back the next night with a big roll of it under his arm. It was blue-purple and very lovely.

"It's velvet," he said. "Did you know that the twilight was velvet? I didn't. But it is! Feel it!"

"It will make a lovely cloak!" said Thimble, feeling the thick purple velvet. "Thank you, Brownie."

She set to work. She cut out a marvellous cloak that would swing right out round the Princess. She lined it with the silver sky, and it shone and shimmered beautifully. All the time she sewed in the two magic spells.

The spells were tiny beads—there were thousands of them! Thimble had to slip them on her needle and sew them into the lining as she worked.

The cloak would be very magic when she had finished!

And then one day the Wizard Sly-One looked in at the window and saw Thimble busily sewing. He knew at once that the cloak was a very special one, for he could smell magic with his nose, just as a dog can smell meat from a distance.

"Good day, Thimble," he said. "What a wonderful cloak! Who is it for?"

"I shan't tell you," said Thimble. "Please shut the window and go away."

"You don't talk to wizards like that!" said Sly-One, crossly.

"Yes, I do," said Thimble, firmly. "Go away!"

"I can smell magic in that cloak," said the wizard, slyly. "Will you sell it to me?"

"Certainly not," said Thimble. "It's for somebody else!"

"It's for the Princess, isn't it?" said Sly-One, who had been told by an owl that Peronel had been to visit Thimble in the middle of the night.

"I shan't tell you a thing!" said Thimble.

But, all the same, Sly-One found out. He paid a little mouse to go and listen to all that Thimble said to herself—for he knew that Thimble whispered to herself as she worked. So the mean little mouse didn't have much difficulty in finding out the secret.

Thimble whispered as she worked, "This is for the dear Princess! She wants to wear it on Midsummer Night—and then she will know everything and will be able to grant wishes. Oh, what a wonderful cloak it will be!"

The little mouse stayed under Thimble's chair and listened to all her whisperings—and then he ran off to tell Sly-One. He was paid by Sly-One, who gave him three pieces of yellow cheese. He was a horrid little mouse, but of great use to the wizard.

"Oho!" thought Sly-One. "This is splendid!

So that cloak is enchanted! Well—I must get hold of it somehow and wear it myself on Midsummer Night! Then I shall know everything—and I can wish bad things whenever I want to!"

So one spring night he crept to Thimble's little cottage and opened the window. Just beneath the sill, neatly folded, was the cloak, ready to be packed up and sent to the Princess the next day. It shone curiously in the moonlight, for it was really very magic indeed.

The wizard carefully dragged the shining cloak out of the window. He shut the window—but it creaked, and Thimble woke up. She gave a squeal as she saw Sly-One in the moonlight—and then she gave a much louder scream for she saw that the enchanted cloak was gone!

"You wicked fellow! Bring it back, bring it back!" shouted Thimble, jumping out of the window. But the wizard was gone. He was nowhere to be seen—and neither was the beautiful cloak.

"And I spent so much time and trouble making it," wept poor Thimble. "Oh, what will the Princess say?"

The Princess was very worried indeed. "Thimble, it wouldn't matter if the cloak hadn't those two spells in it," she said. "You see, I could do a lot of good with that cloak—but Sly-One will do bad things. How can we get it back?"

Sly-One didn't mean them to get it back. He put it away safely in a room right at the very top of his castle, in a tower that had no windows and no chimney—only a great door that he could lock with three different keys.

Sly-One packed the cloak into a box and put the box in the middle of the room. If anyone opened the box a bell would ring, and then Sly-One would know that someone had come to get the cloak.

"But no one can get into my castle—and no one can get into that top room—and no one can open the box, for I have the key!" chuckled Sly-One. "There it shall stay until Midsummer Night—then I will shake it out and wear it, and the magic in it will be mine. Ha, the things I will do then!"

The Princess Peronel soon found out where Sly-One had put her enchanted cloak, and she was quite in despair.

"No one, *no* one can get it from there!" she sighed. "It is quite, quite impossible. Whatever shall we do? Think hard, Thimble! It is your fault that it has been stolen, you know. You shouldn't have left it so near the window!"

Thimble was just as upset as the Princess. She sat and thought all day and night long, wondering what in the world could be done about the magic cloak—and then an idea came into her head. She jumped up at once.

"I can't get the cloak back," she cried, "but I can at least make it unwearable for Sly-One! I will have it spoilt so that he cannot wear it!"

"But, Thimble, however can you do that?" asked Peronel, in surprise. "It's impossible! Why, we can't even get into the castle, and we certainly can't get into that top room. There are three keys to lock the door—and Sly-One has all of them tied firmly round his waist."

"All the same, I think I know what to do," said Thimble. "I must call in an army of little creatures which we usually dislike, Princess— but this time they will help us."

"What little creatures?" asked Peronel, in astonishment.

"Clothes-moths!" cried Thimble. "Listen— we'll get hundreds of clothes-moths to creep in somewhere at Sly-One's castle. They can fly up the stairs—and squeeze in through the keyholes— and squash themselves under the lid and into the box where the cloak is."

"And they can lay their eggs there!" cried Peronel, delighted. "And the eggs will turn into grubs, who will gobble up the whole cloak, so that when Sly-One goes to put it on when Mid-summer Night is here he will find there is nothing but holes!"

"Yes!" said Thimble. She clapped her hands and called out a string of magic words. In two minutes a cloud of tiny light-brown moths flew in at her window. Thimble gave her orders, and in a cloud they flew out again.

They flew to the castle. They crept in through cracks and holes here and there, under doors and windows. They flew up the winding stairs to the topmost room. They squeezed below the door and through the three keyholes—and there they were in the three-times-locked room!

They went to the big box in the middle of the floor. The lid was tight-fitting, but they found one small place where they could squeeze in—and in they all went, one by one.

Inside was the wonderful cloak. Each moth chose its own place and laid a batch of eggs. Then they all crept out again and flew off to tell Thimble that her wishes had been obeyed.

Inside the box the eggs hatched out into very tiny grubs. At once they set to work to eat the cloak. All clothes-moth grubs eat clothes of some sort—and these grubs were very hungry indeed. How they ate! How they gobbled! They grew bigger and bigger, fatter and fatter, as they ate the cloak. Only the tiny beads they did not eat, and these fell to the bottom of the box as the grubs ate the cloak.

Midsummer Night came, and Sly-One stamped up the stairs to get out the cloak. Now, at last, he would know everything and would be able to get all his wishes granted. My, what a bad time he would give everyone!

He unlocked the door. He unlocked the box, and then he gave a cry of anger and rage. There was no cloak there!

All that was left of it was a few rags and a handful of tiny beads! The grubs had done their work well! Sly-One did not know that the clothes-moths had been there—he thought that the cloak

had been stolen. In a rage he caught up the box and threw it out of the window—beads, rags, grubs, and all!

The beads were scattered in the wind. The rags flew off, too. The grubs fell into the grass. The box smashed to pieces.

A small rabbit nearby saw all this in great astonishment, and ran off to tell Thimble. How delighted she was! She hurried to collect what beads she could find, for they held the magic spells, and she meant to make another cloak as soon as she could for Peronel.

She is making it now—but she hasn't quite found all the beads that got blown away by the wind. So if you find any, keep them carefully, and let her know. Her address is: Miss Thimble Pixie, Oak Tree Corner, Cuckoo Wood, near Fairyland. I hope the second cloak won't be stolen, don't you?

THE TWO NAUGHTY BOYS

ONCE UPON a time there were two boys who lived next door to one another. Their names were Ben and Harry, and they were both as bad as could be!

They used to run up to people's front doors, ring the bell, and run away. They called out rude things to passers-by, and if they saw anyone's bicycle leaning against the kerb they would send it over with a crash! By the time the owner came running out of a nearby shop to see what had happened both boys were away down the street, peeping round the corner.

Now one day their Sunday-school teacher said he was going to give a party for his class. All the boys were pleased because they loved parties and games and nice things to eat. There were eighteen in the class, so it would be fun.

The teacher borrowed a small hall to give the party in. He hung it with streamers and balloons and made it very gay. He got lemonade, currant buns, dough-nuts, biscuits, and sweets, and for every boy a big, red, rosy apple.

The sweets were done up in paper bags, and the apples were piled up on a dish in the middle of the table. There were more bags of sweets and apples than there were boys, but as some of the guests had small brothers and sisters the teacher thought they might have some, too. The boys could take them home to them.

Now Ben and Harry went, of course. They played games and had a fine time. And then they sat down to tea. What a tea they had! You wouldn't believe me if I told you how many buns, dough-nuts, and biscuits they managed to eat between them! And then they discovered that there were more bags of sweets and apples than there were boys.

Ben made up his mind at once. He was going to get an extra bag of sweets for himself some-how, and an extra apple! He ate all his own sweets and apple, and then watched to see when he could take another without being seen.

He soon managed to. He slipped the bag of sweets into his pocket, and an apple into another pocket. He grinned to himself in glee to think how clever he had been. He didn't think how mean and dishonest he was.

Now when Harry came up to speak to Ben, Ben couldn't stop himself from telling Harry how clever he had been.

"I've got an extra bag of sweets to take home, and a great big apple!" he whispered. "I've got them in my pocket. Ha, ha! You didn't think of doing that, did you? I'm cleverer than you are!"

Harry was cross. Why hadn't he thought of doing that? He didn't dare to go and take some for himself, because he was afraid of being caught. How could he get some? What could he do? He stood and thought for a while—and then he saw that the conjurer had come into the room, ready to do magic for the boys. He left Ben and ran to get a good seat right in the front. He loved watching a conjurer.

Now whilst he was watching the conjurer an extraordinary idea came into his head. He had thought of a way to get a bag of sweets and an apple for himself, and to make Ben give up his!

So, half-way through the conjurer's performance Harry stood up.

"Please, sir," he said to the conjurer, "I can do magic, too."

"Can you really, my boy!" said the conjurer. "Well, that's fine. What can you do?"

"I can make a bag of sweets and an apple jump from my pockets to the pockets of another boy," said Harry.

"Oh, I don't really think you can do that!" said the conjurer, laughing.

"I can, sir!" said Harry. "Just you watch!"

He took a bag of sweets from the table nearby

and a big red apple. He put the sweets into his left-hand pocket, and the apple into the opposite one. He went up on to the stage.

"Well, do your trick," said the conjurer. "We all saw you put the sweets and apple into your pockets. Now send them into the pockets of another boy!"

Harry looked round for the conjurer's wand. He thought it would look a real magic trick if he waved that in the air! "May I use your wand, please?" said Harry.

"Certainly," said the conjurer. "But I'm afraid it's only magic when *I* use it—so don't expect it to do anything marvellous for *you*!"

"Oh, I expect it will!" said Harry. He picked up the silver wand. Then he turned to face the surprised boys. He showed them the bag of sweets in one pocket and the apple in the other. "Now watch!" he said.

He waved the wand. "Sweets and apple, disappear from my pockets and go into Ben's!" he cried. "Quick, go to Ben!"

Ben went red. He knew perfectly well what Harry was doing. "You stand up, Ben, and go on to the stage!" cried the watching boys. "Go on! Turn out your pockets, and let's see if Harry has done a real magic trick."

Ben had to go up on to the stage. The conjurer put his hand into Ben's pockets—and, of course, pulled out a bag of sweets and a red apple! That was not at all surprising, as you know, because Ben had put them there himself.

But all the boys really thought that the sweets and apple had flown somehow from Harry's pockets into Ben's, and they were most astonished. They didn't for one moment think that sweets and an apple were also in Harry's pockets. Oh, no—they felt sure that the ones taken from Ben's were the same that they had seen Harry take. So they yelled, and cheered, and clapped for all they were worth, and Harry bowed and looked very

pleased. But Ben frowned and scowled, and was in a great temper.

"Well, well," said the conjurer, quite surprised himself. "That's a very clever trick. I'm not at all sure that I would be able to do it myself. Now, boys, what do you say to giving our friend Harry the sweets and apple for himself, as he has done such a good trick for us?"

"Yes, yes!" shouted all the boys. So, to Harry's delight, the sweets and apple taken from Ben's pockets were given to him.

"Golly! Now I've got two lots!" thought Harry, in delight, putting them deep into his pockets. "This is fine. Ben thought he was clever—but I'm twice as clever as he is!"

"Well, now, shall we get on with the show?" said the conjurer. "Unless Ben can do a trick as clever as Harry's? But I'm afraid you can't, Ben."

An idea came into Ben's head. Ha! He *could* play a fine trick on mean Harry. He turned to the conjurer with a broad smile.

"Yes, sir, I can do a trick, too," he said.

"And what can you do?" asked the conjurer, thinking that he had suddenly come up against two very surprising boys.

"Well, sir, you saw that bag of sweets and apple that Harry sent from his pockets to mine, didn't you?" said Ben. "Well, he put them into his own pockets, didn't he?—one bag of sweets and one apple. Well, sir, if you'll lend me that magic wand of yours I can turn that bag of sweets into TWO bags, and that one apple into TWO apples!"

"No, no—you really can't do that," said the conjurer, with a laugh.

"Please, sir, I know I can," said Ben. "Do let me try."

"Very well," said the conjurer, and he handed Ben his wand. Ben waved it in the air. Harry stood on the stage and looked angry. Ben knew he had two bags and two apples, the mean thing! And Harry couldn't do anything about it.

"Bag of sweets, turn into TWO!" shouted Ben, making everyone jump. "Rosy apple, turn into TWO!"

The conjurer went to Harry. He slipped his hand into first one pocket and then the other— and, hey presto, he brought out *two* bags of sweets, of course, and *two* apples! He simply couldn't understand it. Neither could the sixteen watching boys. They stared with wide eyes.

"Goodness! Who would have thought that

Ben and Harry were such marvellous conjurers!" said one boy.

Now the only person who was at all doubtful about the marvellous conjuring was the Sunday-school teacher. He knew Ben and Harry very well indeed, and he felt quite certain that neither of the boys knew anything about conjuring at all. So he sat and thought for a moment or two—and, knowing what naughty boys they were, he felt perfectly certain that one of them must have stolen the sweets and apple first, and made the other envious—and that was how the conjuring began!

"So that's it, is it!" thought the teacher. "Well, I shall see that neither of those naughty boys takes an extra bag of sweets or an apple home."

So when the boys went off the stage the teacher quietly took the two bags of sweets and the apples himself, and gave them to John, who had two brothers at home. Ben and Harry glared at him—they had hoped to have them themselves!

But they had to go home without them. They left the hall together, and as soon as they were safely out of hearing of their teacher they began to quarrel.

"You mean thing! Doing that trick and making

the conjurer find my sweets and apple!" cried Ben.

"Well, you're even meaner! You made him take *all* of them away from me!" cried Harry.

"I'll hit you if you talk to me like that!" cried Ben.

"Well, I'll hit you first!" shouted Harry, and he gave Ben a punch on the arm. Then, of course, they began to fight, and you really should have seen them! Biff, smack, slap, punch! It was dreadful.

Then Ben slipped and fell into the mud. Harry fell on top of him. They rolled into a ditch and caught their coats on some barbed wire. When They got up they found that their clothes were muddy and torn—and they were wearing their best suits, too!

They didn't fight any more, but crept home, hoping that their mothers wouldn't see them. But Ben's mother caught *him*, and Harry's father caught *him*.

Ben was spanked and sent to bed, and Harry was made to empty his money-box to pay for the cleaning and mending of his suit, and *he* was sent to bed, too!

They met again the next day, very sad and sorry, and rather ashamed.

"It was all because I did a mean thing," said Ben. "I shan't behave like that again."

"Well, maybe I won't, either," said Harry.

Perhaps they won't—but they'll find it hard work to behave well after being two such naughty boys!

THE FAT TEDDY-BEAR

THERE WAS once a teddy-bear who ate so much that he became very fat indeed.

"You look as if you will burst out of your brown skin," said the golliwog.

"You really are getting disgustingly fat," said the golden-haired doll.

"I would rather you didn't ride in my carriage any more," said the engine. "I'm afraid you are too fat and heavy."

"Stop being greedy and you won't grow so fat," said the blue cat.

But the bear took no notice of all these remarks. He just went on eating and eating. He knew where the children's cake-tin was, and he could quite easily take off the lid and nibble the cake. He could take off the lid of the biscuit-jar, too. So he could take a biscuit whenever he liked, which was very wrong of him.

Now one day some new soldiers came to live in the nursery. They had fine swords, and they were very proud of them indeed. But the old lead soldiers didn't like the new ones at all. They thought them very vain and proud.

"Keep out of our way or we shall shoot you," said the old lead soldiers, who had guns over their shoulders.

"Don't dare to talk to *us* like that!" said the captain of the new soldiers. "We could run you through with our swords in a trice!"

The toys were quite upset to hear this kind of quarrelling going on, for they had been very peaceful and happy together in the nursery. They tried to stop the soldiers from squabbling, but it wasn't a bit of good.

When the old soldiers took their nightly march round the nursery they usually found that the new ones wanted to go in exactly the same place—across the hearth-rug, round the carpet, and over by the toy-cupboard. It was most annoying.

And when the new soldiers wanted to practise drilling, the old soldiers were sure to be doing exercises in the very spot that the captain of the new soldiers had chosen for his men. It was really tiresome!

Now one night the two armies met as they marched round the nursery, and neither of them would give way. "Go back!" the captain of the new soldiers ordered the old ones.

"Certainly not! *You* go back!" shouted the old soldiers. And then the watching toys were horrified to see that the two armies were about to fight.

The old soldiers took their guns off their shoulders and aimed them at the enemy. The new soldiers drew their sharp swords and brandished them above their heads with shouts.

"Good gracious! I believe they really are going to fight one another!" said the golden-haired doll, in fright.

"I hope they won't kill each other," said the golliwog. He ran up to them.

"Don't fight! Don't be silly!" he begged. But all the soldiers yelled at him.

"Get away, Golly! Don't interfere or you will be hurt!"

All the toys went into the toy-cupboard to watch from a safe place. Only the fat teddy-bear was missing. He had spied the biscuit-jar on the table and had climbed up to get a biscuit. He was munching it when he heard all the noise and excitement down below. He ran to the edge of the table and peeped down.

When he saw that a battle was about to begin he felt most excited. "Good gracious! This is a marvellous place to watch it from," thought the bear. "But what a pity the soldiers are going to fight one another—they may break each other to pieces, and then they will be put into the dustbin."

The old soldiers rushed at the new soldiers, and

such a shouting arose on the air that the golliwog was really afraid the children would hear it. The teddy-bear was terribly excited. He leaned right over the edge of the table to see everything that was happening.

He leaned too far. He felt himself falling! He dropped his biscuit and clutched hold of the table-cloth. But that didn't save him! No—down he went, and down—and, alas for the poor bear, he fell with a great clatter right in the very middle of the old and new soldiers!

He fell on their swords, he fell on their guns. The swords and the guns were only small, of course, but they pricked the poor teddy-bear and made holes in his tight brown skin. He growled and groaned and hit out with his paws as he felt the pricks.

The soldiers were simply terrified when the bear fell down on top of them. They threw away their guns, they threw away their swords, and rushed off to their boxes, squealing in fright.

"It's an earthquake!"

"It's a giant!"

"It's a monster!"

The toys saw the poor teddy groaning on the floor, and they ran to help him up. "Have you hurt yourself?" asked the golliwog, kindly.

The teddy stood up and shook himself—and, to the great horror of the toys, they saw little spurts of sawdust coming out of the holes that the swords and guns had made in the skin of the teddy-bear!

"Gracious!" said the golden-haired doll. "How dreadful! You are leaking your sawdust all over the place, Teddy!"

The bear looked down. He saw little trickles of sawdust coming out of him everywhere, and he was frightened. It was on the floor in little heaps. Whatever was he to do?

He walked a few steps and more sawdust trickled out.

"I say, Teddy, you are going quite thin already," said the golly. "Really you are. Be careful, do. If you lose all your sawdust you will be nothing but brown skin."

"Well, what am I to DO?" wailed the bear. "I can't stop the sawdust from trickling out, can I?"

"Where's nurse's work-basket?" asked the golden-haired doll, suddenly. "I may be able to sew up your holes, Bear."

She found a tiny needle and some brown cotton. She went to the bear and began to sew up each hole. How he squealed when she sewed him! But, really, it was the only thing to do.

At last all the little holes were sewn up, and the bear could walk without sawdust leaking out of him everywhere. But he looked very funny because he was now quite thin. He had lost so much sawdust that his body was different.

"Oh! You look quite nice now," said the golliwog. "You looked so terribly fat before."

"And let me warn you that if you get fat again you will split open the holes I have sewn up, and you will lose more sawdust than ever," said the doll, solemnly.

The bear was frightened to hear this. "I'll never be greedy again," he said. "Never. As for those soldiers who pricked me like that, I'll just go over and say a few stern words to them."

So he did, and they shook in their boots to hear him. They became friends after that, and did their marching and their drilling together.

As for the bear, I saw him the other day. He isn't a bit fat—just nice, really—so I shouldn't think he is greedy any more, would you?

THE CAPTURE OF THE BOLD, BAD BROWNIE

ONCE THERE was a bold, bad brownie called Pouncer. This was a good name for him, because he certainly did pounce out at people!

He liked to lie in wait for the little pixies and fairies who used the paths in Whispering Wood. They often used to carry home their shopping— little pots of honey, new dresses, and tunics made of leaves and gossamer, boxes of sweets from the Sugar Shop, and things like that.

Pouncer would hide behind a bush and wait. Then, when he heard someone coming along, he would pounce on them, take away their goods, and run off down the secret paths that he knew. No one knew where he hid, and no one dared to follow and find out.

Now the smallest pixie of all was the one that Pouncer sprang out on nearly every day. Poor little Lightfoot lost nearly all his shopping, and often had to go without cake or honey for days on end.

"You are a horrid brownie!" he said a dozen

times a month to Pouncer. "No one likes you. One day you'll be caught and punished!"

But Pouncer only laughed his horrid loud laugh and ran away down his own secret paths into the heart of Whispering Wood. Then Lightfoot would go home, empty-handed, feeling very sad.

Everyone liked little Lightfoot. He was as gay as the big butterflies that floated overhead, and as merry as the grasshoppers that jumped in the fields.

The insects all loved him because he was never too busy to talk to them. He spoke to the furry caterpillars and told them where their favourite food was. He made the big snails come out of their shell-houses and go for long, slow walks

with him, leaving behind a silvery trail. He called to the spiders and asked them for bits of their thin, strong thread whenever he wanted to sew.

"You mustn't call *us* insects," said the spiders, who rather looked down on the flies and beetles in the wood. "We are not insects—and neither are the snails."

"I know," said Lightfoot. "I think you are very clever indeed. I do love your wonderful webs. I really do!"

Now one day the spiders heard Lightfoot crying bitterly because Pouncer had once more sprung out at him and taken away his shopping.

"I had two little pots of honey," wept Lightfoot, "and I had a chocolate cake with a little red flower in the middle of it, and I had a new hat with stamens in for feathers. It was sweet. But Pouncer has taken them all away. Oh, how I wish we could capture him and take him prisoner. But nobody knows where he lives—and, even if we did, we wouldn't dare to try and capture him. He's so strong."

The spiders didn't like to see little Lightfoot so unhappy. The big curly snail came up to see what was the matter. He left his silvery trail behind him as he came. "Don't worry," he said. "I've found a lovely toadstool this morning, with a most delicious taste. Come with me and you shall bite it."

Now after Lightfoot had gone home, feeling a bit better, the spiders and the snail talked together.

"It's such a shame that Lightfoot loses so much of his shopping," said the biggest spider, waving one of her eight legs about. "Can't we do something about it?"

"Well, we could follow Pouncer into the wood," said another. "He wouldn't notice spiders, I'm sure. We could find out where his hiding-place is, and attack him."

"What's the good of that?" said another spider. "He could easily beat us off. After all, we are only spiders. And we might get lost. We might not be able to find our way back to the paths we know."

"I know what we could do!" cried the first spider. "We could find a snail somewhere near where Pouncer lives, and send him to tell Lightfoot where the brownie is. You know that snails always leave a silvery trail behind them. Well, Lightfoot and his friends could follow the trail back, and then they could capture the bold, bad brownie."

"That sounds a good idea," said a small spider, scratching her head with one of her many legs. "If only we can keep Pouncer there till Lightfoot and his friends come all together to catch him!"

"Couldn't we wait till the brownie is asleep, and then weave our webs all round him to make a kind of cage?" said the first spider.

"That *would* be a good idea!" cried all the spiders together. "That's what we'll do! Come along—let's watch out for Pouncer and follow him to his home."

So the next time that Pouncer was in that part of the wood, six of the spiders watched out for him. They saw him pounce on little Lightfoot and take his butter and eggs away. Then, in a silent row, the six big spiders followed the bold, bad brownie into the heart of the wood.

T.A.T.   F

Down the secret paths he went, humming a song because he was pleased with himself. He came to a little clearing among the trees, spread with soft green moss. Here he had his hiding-place. He slept each night on the soft moss, and when it rained he put up a big green umbrella that he had stolen from Dame Get-About.

The spiders followed Pouncer quietly. He had no idea that they were behind him. He sat down on the moss and ate a big meal. Then he yawned loudly and lay down. A little finger of sunshine crept through the trees and warmed the moss he was lying on. Pouncer felt very happy and comfortable.

He spoke to a hedgehog running by. "How can you run on such a hot day! I'm going to sleep. That's the thing to do on a hot afternoon like this —sleep on the soft moss in the middle of the Whispering Wood!"

He closed his eyes. His mouth fell open, and he began to snore a little. The six spiders moved forward very quietly on their eight long legs. They surrounded him. Then, at a sign from the biggest one, they began to weave their silken web.

They made a web on each side of him, and they made a web over the top, as a kind of roof. They hung the webs with sticky drops, so that if he tried to escape his legs and arms would get entangled like a fly's—and he wouldn't be able to move!

The webs were soon finished, for all six spiders

worked hard. They were very clever, and the webs were beautiful. When they had done their work they ran a little way back and looked at it.

"It looks just as if Pouncer is in a cage!" said the biggest spider. And, indeed, it did! There he lay in the middle of the five webs, fast asleep and snoring.

"Does anyone remember the way back?" said a spider. But nobody did, because it was a long way to Pouncer's hiding-place.

"Then we will find a snail who knows the way and send *him* back," said the spider. So they found a snail hiding under a big stone, and told him to go and find Lightfoot.

This snail was cousin to the one that Lightfoot so often spoke to, and he was quite willing to go and find the little Pixie. He set off slowly, leaving behind him the broad silvery trail.

He came to Lightfoot at last, and called to him. "Lightfoot! Lightfoot! The six big spiders have captured Pouncer. They have got him a cage made of webs, and they have sent me to tell you to come and get him. Then you can put him into prison and punish him for all the bad things he has done!"

"But how shall I know the way to where Pouncer lives?" cried Lightfoot.

"I have left you my broad, silvery trail to follow," said the snail. "You cannot miss it, Lightfoot. Go quickly, because I have been a long time coming, and soon the sun will go down and the woods will be dark."

Lightfoot called his friends to him and told them what the snail had said. Joyfully they followed Lightfoot into the heart of the Whispering Wood.

"At last we can capture the bold, bad brownie and punish him!" they cried. "No longer will he be able to lie in wait for us and rob us of our goods!"

Lightfoot could easily see the silvery trail that

the snail had left. He followed it, and after a time he and his friends came to where the six spiders were waiting patiently. Pouncer was still asleep in the middle of the cage of webs.

Lightfoot and the others cried out in surprise to see such a fine cage. "How clever you are!" they said to the spiders. "Pouncer can't possibly escape!"

Pouncer heard the voices and awoke. He sat up and gazed in amazement at the webs around him. Then he saw the pixie and his friends, and jumped to his feet in a rage.

"Oho! So you think you can capture me, do you!" he shouted, angrily. "Well, you can't! I won't let you tie me with ropes and lead me away! Not I!"

He rushed away, but the webs caught him and he felt his arms and legs and head all tangled up in the sticky threads. He tried to free himself, but the more he struggled the faster the webs held him. At last he sank to the ground, quite tired out, his arms and legs held fast by the spider-threads.

"He's tied himself up in the webs!" cried the pixie, joyfully. "We can easily take him back now!"

So they carried Pouncer back through the secret paths, following the snail's silvery trail once more. And Pouncer was shut up in a hollow tree for a whole year, and only allowed out when he promised faithfully never to be bold or bad again.

The year is up to-morrow. Pouncer will be free, and he is going to leave the Whispering Wood and start again somewhere else. He doesn't want to be bold and bad any more!

Weren't the spiders and the snail clever? You can see the snail's silvery trail any morning if you look around your garden. Find one and see how easy it was for Lightfoot to follow it. And look at the beautiful spiders' webs and you'll know just what Pouncer's cage looked like when it was made. I wouldn't have liked to be caught inside it, would you?

SHE LOST HER MEMORY!

THERE WAS once a little girl whom everyone called Dolly Daydreams. You can guess why. She was such a little dreamer that she just forgot everything she was told.

When her mother said to her, "Now don't forget to bring back your slippers from school, Dolly," do you suppose she ever remembered? No—she might bring back someone else's handkerchief by mistake, but she certainly wouldn't bring back her slippers!

Sometimes her teacher said to her, "Dolly, to-morrow I want you to remember to bring me some dandelions for the Nature lesson," and Dolly would nod her golden head and say, "Yes, Miss Brown" at once.

But she wouldn't remember to bring the dande-lions.

One day her mother said, "Dolly! I am really afraid you will forget to bring your head back with you one day. Just see it is on your shoulders, will you, each morning you leave school?"

Well, it was lucky for Dolly that her head was tightly fixed to her shoulders, or she certainly would have left it behind if she could. Everyone laughed at her, but her teacher looked rather solemn.

"You have such a bad memory that one day, if you are not careful, I'm afraid you will lose it altogether," said Miss Brown. "Yes, I'm really afraid of that, Dolly. Then you won't be able to remember anything at all!"

Well, one afternoon, when Dolly was coming home from school, she sat down under the hedge to rest. And a small man peeped out from under a big thistle and spoke to her.

"Little girl! Your memory has come loose. It's almost falling off you. Hadn't you better do something about it?"

Dolly laughed. "Don't be silly," she said. "Memories don't come loose."

"Oh yes, they do, if you don't look after them," said the little man. "I can see yours quite clearly hanging loose."

Dolly looked all round herself, but she couldn't see anything at all. She felt quite sure that the little man was making it all up. She tossed her golden head.

"I'm all right!" she said. "I could remember anything if I really tried—but it's too much bother."

"Ah—that's why you are losing your memory, then," said the little man, wisely. "One day you will, little girl. Well, if you ever do, come to me and I may be able to help you. Here is my name and address. Tuck it away carefully in your pocket."

He gave Dolly a small card. She looked at it. On it was written, "Rufus Remember, Under the Big Thistle, Farmer Bates's Cornfield."

"What a funny name and address!" said Dolly, putting it into her pocket. "All right—I'll come and ask you for help if I ever do lose my memory altogether, but that's quite impossible!"

Well, the little man was perfectly right—Dolly's memory was very loose indeed, and on the

way home through Primrose Wood she lost it
altogether. It just dropped out of her head and
fell down into a clump of violets. She didn't
notice it at all.

But after a bit she stood still and tried to think.
"Where am I going? Where is my home? I
can't remember where I'm going!"

She felt queer. This wasn't nice at all. She
felt sure she was going home, but she couldn't
remember where her home was—and she couldn't
remember who her mother was either. A horrid
cold feeling crept into her heart. "Mummy! I

want to go home to you—but I can't remember where you live, or who you are!"

Dolly began to cry, for she didn't know whether to go straight on, or turn back, or what to do! A

big boy came along, whistling. He stopped when he saw Dolly crying.

"What's the matter?" he asked. "Have you hurt yourself? Shall I take you home?"

"I don't know where my home is," said Dolly, sadly.

"Well, what's your name?" asked the big boy.

"If you tell me that, maybe I can find out where you live and take you."

But, alas! Poor little Dolly couldn't remember her own name! She tried and she tried, but it was no good. She stood staring up at the big boy, and he grew impatient with her.

"Well, hurry up—surely you know your own name!" he cried.

"I can't remember it!" said Dolly, and she cried such big tears down her cheeks that the boy was quite astonished.

"Well, I do think you are a little silly," he said, "not to know your own name! Well, really! I can't stop any more. I'm late already. You just walk on through the wood until you remember your name. I think you're just being rather a baby."

He went off, whistling. Dolly felt very lonely. She walked on a little way, and met an old cottage-woman coming along with a bag of shopping.

"What's the matter with you?" asked the old lady, in surprise. "Where do you come from?"

"I don't know," sobbed Dolly.

"Oh, don't be silly!" said the old woman, putting down her bag. "What's your name?"

"I don't know. I've forgotten it," said Dolly.

"I've forgotten where I live, too—and I've forgotten who my Mummy is, though I remember her kind face very well. And I want to get back home to her."

"What school do you go to?" asked the old woman, quite puzzled at Dolly's answers.

"I don't know," said Dolly. "I just don't know anything! I don't know where I am."

"Well, you *are* a funny little girl!" said the old woman. "Have you any brothers or sisters? If you tell me their names I may know them and can take you home."

"I don't know if I have or not," said Dolly, trying to remember. "I just can't remember at all. Somebody told me that my memory was coming loose, and I didn't believe them. Oh dear!—if only I had, I might have done something about it. But now it's too late. I've forgotten everything."

"Dear me, this is very serious," said the old woman. "Just wait whilst I go and put my shopping away, and I'll come and take you to the police-station. Maybe the policeman there will know who you are."

She went into a nearby cottage. But as soon as she had gone Dolly forgot all about her. She wandered off, going back the way she had come.

She tried to remember what day it was, but she couldn't. She tried to remember if she had been at school that day—but no, she couldn't even remember that.

She put her hand into her pocket to get out her

hanky to wipe her eyes—and she felt something hard there. She took it out. It was the little card that the tiny man in the hedge had given to her. Dolly read it in surprise, for she had quite forgotten all about the little man by now.

"Rufus Remember, Under the Big Thistle,

Farmer Bates's Cornfield," she read. "How extraordinary! I must go and find him, because he must be somebody I know. Maybe he could tell me who I am!"

Dolly met a little girl about her own age, and she spoke to her. "Please could you tell me which is Farmer Bates's Cornfield?"

"Yes—just go through that gate," said the little girl, and ran off. Dolly went through the gate and found herself in the cornfield. She looked about for a big thistle. At first she couldn't see one at all, and then, in the ditch under the hedge, she saw a very big one indeed. Perhaps that was the right one!

She went to it and looked underneath—but there was nobody there. She called aloud: "Rufus Remember! Rufus Remember! Are you anywhere about?"

The little man popped round by a big nettle and looked up at Dolly's tear-stained face in surprise.

"You're soon back again," he said. "What's the matter?"

"Oh, have I been here before?" said Dolly, in astonishment. "Rufus Remember, can you help me? Do you know who I am? What's my name?"

"I've no idea," said Rufus Remember. "Dear me, so your loose memory got lost after all, I suppose? I felt sure it would. But you wouldn't believe me. It's a very serious thing to lose a perfectly good memory, you know."

"What can I do about it?" asked Dolly.

"Well, I've got one I can let you have, but it's a fairy's memory, not a proper person's," said Rufus. "So you'll think of all kinds of queer things sometimes, you know—moonlight dances in the woods, queer spells that only fairies know, and on Midsummer Night you'll have to come out into the woods and curtsey to the Fairy Queen."

"Oooh—I shan't mind that!" said Dolly. "Please give me that memory, Rufus."

"Bend down," said Rufus.

So Dolly bent down. Rufus parted her hair and then took something from a very tiny box. He pressed it into Dolly's head and she gave a little squeal. "Oooooh! Something's gone into my head."

"It's your new memory," said Rufus. "Now—do you know who you are?"

"Yes, I'm Dolly," said the little girl. "And my Mummy is Mrs. Dawson. And I live in Rose Cottage. I remember everything!"

"Now you must remember this one thing I am going to tell you," said Rufus. "A fairy's memory, which is what I've given you, is a very delicate thing, and you have to guard it carefully, or it will fade away. You must never, never be careless or lazy—you must always remember everything you are told. Will you?"

"Oh yes," said Dolly, happily. "I'll do my very best now. I've had a dreadful lesson. I'll never forget things again."

She ran home, and although she was scolded for being late, she didn't tell anyone the reason. She was sure they wouldn't believe her if she told them she had lost her own memory and been given a fairy's instead. I do hope she keeps it and doesn't let it fade away, don't you?

A SURPRISE FOR MOLLIE

THE CHILDREN were in the nursery, playing with their toys, when Mummy called to them.

"Alan! Mollie! You really must go out into the garden this nice sunny day! Hurry now!"

"Oh, Mummy—just a minute!" cried Mollie. "I'm putting my doll to bed. She's got measles."

"Well, it would be better to take her out in her pram, a nice day like this," said Mummy, coming into the nursery.

"Mummy, it would be dangerous," said Mollie.

"Alan's the doctor, and he told me to keep Angela in bed for two days. Please just let me finish tucking her up."

"Very well," said Mummy. "Then go out and play till I call you in for lunch. And come in with good appetites, please, because there will be egg-salad—and for a treat you may have a very little cucumber!"

"Ooooh!" said the children. They loved egg-salad, and they thought cucumber was so cool to eat, though they were not allowed very much.

"There will be juicy little tomatoes, too," said Mummy. "So come in as soon as you hear the dinner-bell."

Mollie finished putting her doll to bed. Angela's bed was a big cardboard box that Mummy had lined for her with some pink padded silk. Mummy had made her a pillow, too, and Mollie herself had made the little sheets and blankets. Angela really looked sweet in the bed.

"Hurry up," said Alan, impatiently. "I want to play Red Indians. You *are* a time, Mollie!"

"I'm ready now," said Mollie, and she stood up. "Good-bye, Angela, dear. I hope you will go to sleep."

The two children went out into the sunny garden. It was lovely out there. The sun was

warm, the bees were humming, and the sparrows were chirping madly.

"Now we're Red Indians," said Alan. "Here's a spear for you. We'll hide in the bushes and jump out if an enemy comes."

It took them all the morning to play their game, and they were hot, hungry, and tired at the end of it. They were pleased to hear the dinner-bell.

"Good!" said Alan. "Egg-salad—cucumber— lettuce, and radishes, I expect—and little juicy tomatoes out of the greenhouse. Hurrah!"

They ran in. Mummy called to them from the nursery, where she was busy setting out the lunch. "Wash your hands and do your hair, please."

They were always supposed to do that before a meal, but they always had to be told! Off they went to wash, and then they brushed their hair neatly.

There came a ring at the front-door bell just then. Mummy had to go and see who it was, and then spend a few minutes talking to the caller. The children were impatient, for they were hungry. They waited in the hall for Mummy. At last she shut the front door and came over to them.

"Well, I'm ready at last," she said. "Come along."

They went upstairs to the nursery. Mummy had set the lunch out on the table by the window. Alan ran over to it. He looked at the salad.

"Oh, Mummy! You said we could have some cucumber—and there isn't a single bit on the dish! And there aren't any tomatoes either."

"Yes, there are," said Mummy. "I put them there myself!"

But when she came over to the table, too, she stared in surprise. Alan was quite right. There wasn't any cucumber, and not a single tomato either!

Mummy turned the salad over with a spoon. No—there really was only lettuce and radishes.

How very queer! Mummy looked at the two children.

"You haven't slipped up here, surely, and eaten the cucumber and tomatoes yourselves?" she asked.

"Of *course* not, Mummy!" cried both children, at once. "You know we wouldn't."

Mummy looked all round the nursery as if to see who could possibly have taken some of the salad. "It's most extraordinary," she said. "No bird would come and steal the cucumber and tomatoes—and certainly no cat or dog would. Then who in the world has taken them?"

Alan and Mollie looked all round the nursery, too, but they couldn't see anyone or anything that might have stolen their salad. But Mollie suddenly noticed something that made her cry out in surprise.

"Who's thrown Angela out of her bed? Look —poor darling, she's lying on the floor, face downwards—and she's ill with the measles, too. Alan—did you do that?"

"No, I didn't," said Alan. "Of course I didn't. Aren't I Angela's doctor? Would I throw a patient out of her bed on to the floor? Don't be silly."

"Well, who did, then?" cried Molly. She ran over to her doll and picked her up.

"Mollie, you really must come and have lunch now," said Mummy, thinking that Mollie would be a long time tucking her doll up in bed again. "Come along now. You can see to Angela afterwards."

"Oh, Mummy just let me put her into her bed," said Mollie. She put her hand on the little blankets to pull them back—and then she gave such a squeal that Mummy and Alan almost jumped out of their seats.

"Ooooooooooh! There's somebody in my doll's bed! Look! Look! What is it?"

Mummy and Alan ran to see. And whatever do you suppose was lying fast asleep in the little bed? You would never, never guess, I'm sure! It was a small brown monkey, curled up under the sheets, his head on the pillow, fast asleep!

"Is he real?" said Alan. "Yes—he must be. He's breathing. Oh, Mollie—I do think he's rather sweet."

"Why—he must be Major Beeton's pet monkey!" cried Mummy, in the greatest surprise. "I met him this morning, and he told me the little thing had escaped. You know, he is usually kept in a big cage, and he has a little basket in the cage, with a pillow and blankets that he rolls himself in. That's why he has cuddled down into your doll's bed, Mollie. It reminded him of his own little basket."

"Well, he shouldn't have thrown poor Angela out," said Mollie. "Mummy, doesn't he look funny in my doll's bed?"

"Mummy, was it the monkey who took our cucumber and tomatoes from the salad?" asked Alan, suddenly. "Do monkeys like them?"

"Of course!" said Mummy. "He must have looked in at the window and seen our nice lunch on the table. And he just helped himself to what he liked the most! Then he wanted to sleep, and found himself a bed."

"I like him," said Alan. "I wish we could keep him. If Mollie didn't want him to sleep in her doll's bed I would let him have my big bicycle basket."

"I expect Major Beeton will want him back," said Mummy. "Shut the window, will you, Alan. And you shut the door, Mollie. Then if he wakes he can't get out. I'll go and telephone to Major Beeton."

Mummy went off to the phone. The children shut the door and the window. Mummy soon came back.

"Major Beeton is delighted that we have found Marmaduke," said Mummy.

"Oh, is that his name?" asked Alan. "Doesn't it suit him, Mummy! Marmaduke, the monkey. It's lovely."

Marmaduke woke up when he heard his name. He sat up in bed and looked at the children and Mummy. Then he jumped out, ran to the table, and climbed up on Mollie's knee. She was so pleased that she could hardly speak.

"Oh, I wish we could keep him," she said. "I do like him so. I love my dolls and my other toys—but they don't run about and climb on my knee like Marmaduke."

Marmaduke behaved himself very well indeed. He took a bit of lettuce from Mollie's plate and nibbled a bit of hard-boiled egg that Alan gave him. He loved the ripe plum that Mummy took from the dish on the nursery dresser, and the children thought he was very clever when he carefully took off the skin before eating it. He was rather rude about the stone, though. He spat it out on the floor.

"He ought to belong to us, really," said Alan,

picking up the stone. "We could teach him his manners."

When Major Beeton came to get his monkey the children were sad.

"We do wish we could have him," said Mollie. "You know, Major Beeton, he hasn't got very beautiful manners—but I'm sure he could learn."

"Well, you come and teach him some, then," said Major Beeton. "Come to tea with me each week, and we'll have old Marmaduke out of his cage. You shall play with him and teach him as many manners as you like. But I'm not sure he'll learn them!"

The children were simply delighted. They are going to tea with Marmaduke to-morrow—and what do you think Mollie has got as a present for him? One of her doll's best hats, trimmed with a red feather. Won't Marmaduke look fine!

TALES AFTER TEA